**E-mail from: Mitch Kannon, fire chief,
Turning Point, Texas
To: Dan Egan, fire chief, Courage Bay, California**

I had to weigh in with my conscience on this one, Dan, but I promised to let you know how things were going with the volunteers you sent down.

What's got me concerned is that I've lost track of your emergency nurse, Cheryl Tierney. She's a real professional, that one, and since she'd pretty much finished setting up the triage area in our temporary shelter, I sent her out on a call. Went to splint a little kid's arm a few miles out of town.

Rain's coming down like I've never seen it before, and visibility's poor. The family she went to help said Cheryl left there a while ago and was headed for a shortcut back to town. Trouble is, the shortcut crossed over a bridge, and news is that the bridge washed out.

I'm not too worried. I figure Cheryl's holed up somewhere safe to wait out the storm. I'm hoping she might have made it as far as Noah Arkin's place. Noah's our local vet, and if she's with him, he and his menagerie will keep her safe. The power's starting to go out in places and cell phone service is spotty, but as soon as I get word on Cheryl, I'll let you know come hell or high water.

About the Author

CAROL MARINELLI

was born in England and following her nursing training
worked for a number of years in a phenomenally busy
Accident and Emergency department. Taking a year
off to backpack around Australia had rather more far
reaching consequences than Carol had anticipated:
marriage, three wonderful children and emigration
(not in that order!).

Writing had always been a dream, though one she'd
never quite followed through on. With her husband's
endless encouragement, gradually the story that had
lived in her head for way too long found a new home
on her computer and finally became her first book.
Now she writes for Medical Romance and Presents
and is thrilled to have been asked to write a book
for the wonderful Code Red series!

code RED

CAROL MARINELLI

WASHED AWAY

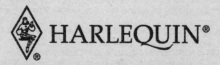

HARLEQUIN®

TORONTO • NEW YORK • LONDON
AMSTERDAM • PARIS • SYDNEY • HAMBURG
STOCKHOLM • ATHENS • TOKYO • MILAN • MADRID
PRAGUE • WARSAW • BUDAPEST • AUCKLAND

HARLEQUIN BOOKS
225 Duncan Mill Road, Don Mills,
Ontario, Canada M3B 3K9

ISBN 0-373-61298-2

WASHED AWAY

Copyright © 2004 by Harlequin Books S.A.

Carol Marinelli is acknowledged as the author of this work

www.eHarlequin.com

Printed in U.S.A.

Dear Reader,

Writing can be lonely at times, so I was thrilled to work with so many wonderful authors on the Code Red series. It has been a real roller-coaster ride for me—getting to know not just my own hero and heroine, but my coauthors', as well. On top of that, I loved corresponding with the other authors and working out all the little nuances of the interlinked characters that made them so real. In fact, by the time I'd finished the book, they were so real to me, I half expected to meet them walking down the street!

I was equally thrilled to finally have a valid excuse (if ever I needed one!) to travel from Australia, where I live, to America and finally witness firsthand all the wonderful images that I'd only seen from my television screen.

On the downside, I've now got permanently itchy feet and miss the buzz of working on a linked series.

Still, I've got the other fifteen books to add to my "to-be-read pile," which can only mean a happy ending!

Happy reading,
Carol Marinelli

For Damian, Ronnie, Hagen,
Erin and Lara Burns.
With love and thanks.

CHAPTER ONE

"YOU KNOW WHAT this is called, don't you, Cheryl?" Chief Mitch Kannon asked as he walked into the fire station headquarters, where a lonesome Cheryl Tierney was rather dispiritedly stocking a shelf with bandages in the makeshift triage area she was setting up—alone.

Cheryl and three other volunteers had flown in from Courage Bay, California, to Turning Point, Texas, to help receive the massive number of evacuees from the more northerly city of Corpus Christi, where a category four hurricane was due to hit.

All four of them had put their hands up without question when the request for assistance came in. All four of them had been keen to get there, ready for action the minute they arrived. They were emergency personnel after all. This was the type of drama they lived for!

And three of them were already out there in the thick of it. They'd been sent out on calls by Mitch, which left Cheryl to set up the area, alone and frustrated.

Cheryl gave a small shrug in response to Mitch's question; she had no idea what he was going on about. Maybe another lecture was about to ensue. She'd barely set foot in Turning Point, a touch shaken after a turbulent flight but more than ready to get started, only to be told by the fire chief in no uncertain terms that the operating room scrubs and runners she was wearing weren't "suitable" wet-weather gear. He'd promptly handed her a massive oversize pair of navy trousers and a cotton shirt that had seen better days, topped off with a huge pair of woolly socks and steel-toe boots—which she'd quickly changed into—then headed to the chief's briefing. Mitch had instructed the gathered emergency teams as to their various roles and the types of damage and injuries they were to expect when the category four hurricane hit. She'd accepted his directions about the triage area for the expected casualties without question, and even smiled sweetly when Turning Point's retired school nurse, Florence Templeton, who was eighty if she was a day, had chided her about the way she folded blankets. But if Mitch Kannon was about to offer advice on how to set up the equipment in *her* triage area, then he had better brace himself for a less-than-welcome response.

Cheryl was an experienced trauma nurse, exactly what Mitch Kannon had requested when he'd called on his old friend and colleague Fire Chief Dan Egan in Courage Bay and asked for a crack team to be sent. Advice about her clothes and her role in the disaster plan Cheryl would happily take, but if the fire chief was about to tell her how to stock the triage area, then it had better be with reasons he could back up. Trauma was Cheryl's baby; emergency nursing was what she did best in this world, and she'd argue her side of things till she was blue in the face if that was what it took.

"I'll tell you what they call this, Cheryl," Mitch carried on easily, ignoring her rigid movements as she continued setting up. "This is what they call the lull before the storm."

He laughed loudly at his lame joke, and for the first time since arriving in Turning Point, Cheryl found herself warming to the man.

Smiling even.

Since Dan Egan had called her, Cheryl had been running on pure adrenaline, but as the hours ticked by and everyone except her was out on a call, she was beginning to feel curiously deflated.

Nate Kellison, a paramedic with the Courage Bay fire department, had been sent to assist in the delivery of a baby. His colleague, Dana Ivie, a firefighter and Emergency Medical Technician was flying off to search for a group of Boy Scouts and their leader who'd been involved in a car accident. And ER resident Amy Sherwood, who'd been helping Cheryl, had set out with the sheriff, Jessie Boone, to assess the rescue center for evacuees that was located in the local high school.

Cheryl would love to be dealing with any one of those assignments, yet here she was, still setting up the triage area. The only other thing she'd done was give a couple of firefighters their tetanus boosters.

"I've been ordered to take a coffee break," Mitch told her.

"I thought you were the one who gave the orders around here."

"Usually." Mitch grinned. "But when Ruth, my dispatcher, tells me it's time for a break, I know better than to argue. Come join me for five minutes."

The rain was pounding on the roof now as Cheryl accepted the mug of coffee Mitch was pouring for her from a thermos. She took a sip, screwing up her face as she did so. "No sugar."

"I figured you wouldn't take it." Mitch winked as he pulled a couple of sachets out of his pocket and handed them to her. "A skinny thing like you."

"*Too* skinny," Cheryl corrected. "I need all the sugar I can get, but even I don't carry supplies in my pocket. Although," she added shaking her head as he unwrapped a mountain of a sandwich, "I do bring my own lunch."

"You're not serious." Mitch grinned as Cheryl put down her coffee and rummaged in her backpack pulling out a plastic container. Peeling off the lid, she revealed a large cheese and lettuce sandwich.

"That bread must have taken a whole field just to produce the grains loaded into it," Mitch teased her. "You'll upset the Women's Auxiliary if you go spurning their sandwiches. We do eat in Texas, you know. We were intending to feed the volunteers."

"I know. I just wasn't sure when we'd get time to stop, so I figured it was easier to bring my own. I've got dinner in there somewhere, but don't worry. I'll tell the ladies that their sandwiches are the nicest I've tasted." Her cheeky smile was rewarded with one of Mitch's.

"So what's a girl from New York doing in California?" Mitch asked. "You'll never lose that accent, you know."

"I don't want to," Cheryl admitted, stirring her coffee with the end of a pen, and avoiding the fire chief's eyes, not quite ready to go there at the best of times and certainly not with someone she'd barely met. "Or, you could ask, 'What's a trauma nurse from California doing in Turning Point, Texas?'"

"Good point," Mitch said lightly, realizing she didn't want to talk about her past. But his curiosity was piqued. There was something that didn't add up with Cheryl Tierney. Sure, she seemed to know what she was doing, was poised and assertive as well, and that long dark hair neatly tied back spelt Confidence with a capital *C*. But there was a sadness in those dark brown eyes, a slight aloofness behind that perfect smile that told Mitch all wasn't as well as it seemed. And even though he had plenty of other things to be worrying about today, he was also a dad. Jolene, his daughter, was around the same age as Cheryl, and if he came across as nosey or a bit interfering, Mitch wasn't making apologies. He looked out for his staff, and today, Cheryl was one of them.

"So where in New York are you from?"

"New Rochelle," Cheryl answered stiffly, taking a slug of her coffee and effectively ending the conversation.

"How long have you been in Courage Bay?" Mitch persisted, despite Cheryl's obvious reluctance.

"Two years now," Cheryl answered, obviously feeling safer now that she could shift the conversation to work. "Heading up the trauma room."

"A tough job?"

Cheryl gave a rueful smile. "Which is exactly how I like it."

"What about your parents? Are they still in New Rochelle?" He watched her shoulders stiffen, heard the long pause before she answered way too lightly for a woman with pursed lips.

"My mom is. My dad moved out to…" She gave a tight shrug, took another sip of her coffee. "Look, I'd better get back to it—thanks for bringing the coffee over."

"You haven't even drunk it," Mitch pointed out. "Or eaten your lunch. You're allowed to have a break, you know."

"I can eat and work at the same time," Cheryl responded. "It won't be the first time."

"Take a break while you can, Cheryl. Things will soon pick up."

"I hope so." Cheryl sighed, then checked herself. "Not that I want anyone to get injured or anything," she added.

"Oh, come on, Cheryl," Mitch laughed. "You're a trauma nurse. You get your kicks the same way I do. I've been in this game more years than I care to count, but I still get a thrill when the emergency bell goes, still get that high as we screech out of the station on the way to a fire. It doesn't mean I want someone to be hurt or trapped, but if someone is, then I know one thing for sure—I want to be the guy to help." He shot a look at Cheryl. "Are you gonna try and tell me you don't feel the same?"

"No." Cheryl grinned. "I guess we're just good at what we do, Mitch."

"Which is why you want to be out there," Mitch said perceptively. "Which is why you want to be in the thick of things, not stocking up a few shelves and shuffling around in clothes that don't really fit. Though you'll be glad of them later!"

"I'm sure you're right," Cheryl conceded, warming by the minute to Mitch. He was down-to-earth, straight talking with a sense of humor—but more to the point, he also possessed a quiet air of leadership that demanded respect, and no doubt got it.

Mitch Kannon, Cheryl decided, was the type of guy that got the best out of a team, because, quite simply, he gave it himself. The type of guy who had taken five minutes out of his undoubtedly hectic schedule to get to know a member of the team he was leading, safe in the knowledge he would be rewarded tenfold later.

Cheryl knew that, because it was the way she herself worked.

Okay, she wasn't the social butterfly of Courage Bay Emergency. Truth be told she kept pretty much to herself. But her patients always came first. No hidden agenda, no massaging egos to further her career. She gave her best and expected no less from those around her.

"It's hard to believe we're in the same country sometimes," Mitch sighed. "Thanks for being so good with Florence, by the way. The old school nurse," he added when Cheryl frowned as she tried to place the name. "I've asked her to man the high school where most people are being evacuated to. She's going to deal with minor cuts and bruises once the place starts to fill. I figured she'd be happier over there, and judging by the way she took off, I reckon I was right. Florence might come across as fierce, but she's a sweetheart really. She's been around longer than anyone else I can think of. There's not a single person who lives in Turning Point who hasn't had their heads personally checked by Florence for nits."

"And she makes a mean bed," Cheryl said, "*with* hospital corners."

"The bedspread is so tight you could bounce a dime off it," Mitch agreed. "But she's a good sort, and even if she comes across as bossy, she knows she's not up to dealing with a major incident. She's glad you're here, really."

"You could have fooled me," Cheryl quipped.

"She is," Mitch said firmly. "We all are. This is a great place to live, a great place to raise a family, but at the end of the day, it's a rural community stuck in the middle of nowhere. When trouble happens, everyone's more than willing to pitch in, but sometimes the job's just too big. We get by for the most part using good old common sense, and there's a lot to be said for it, but at times like this, a bit more is needed. The people of Turning Point and Corpus Christi deserve it. This storm's going to devastate a lot of people. That's why I called my old friend Dan Egan and asked him to see about sending help. The only doctor in Turning Point, Dr. Holland, had a heart attack a few weeks ago. He's still in hospital in Houston. I had an EMT on staff but she just moved to North Dakota...."

"Which leaves you and Florence?"

"And a mighty team of volunteers—but you can see

why I'm more than happy to have help arrive. Now, have you got everything you need?" Mitch asked, before draining the last of his coffee in one gulp.

"Pretty much." Cheryl looked around and nodded. "We brought a lot of equipment with us. Mind you, it depends on how many casualties arrive. Amy wanted to see about getting a couple of oxygen saturation monitors from Dr. Holland's clinic, so if someone can get into it and get them, that would be great, and a few more IV poles wouldn't go unused. I've set up some hooks on the back walls, so anyone needing IV therapy will have to stay over there." She pointed to the far wall, and Mitch gave an approving nod.

"You've done an amazing job. It looks like a real minihospital. There's still a bit more equipment to come. Noah, the local veterinarian, is heading over— should be here anytime now. He said he'd bring over some stuff we might need, though don't ask me what. I'll have to leave the medical side of things to you."

Which was just the way Cheryl wanted it.

"Well, so long as he doesn't expect to set up shop here, as well," Cheryl laughed. "I know it's an emergency, but I don't relish the idea of working alongside roaming horses and low-flying birds."

"You don't have to worry. Noah's just bringing the gear over and heading straight back to his clinic. He has his own work cut out for him. I'll go and see about getting someone into Doc Holland's rooms for you."

"That would be great." Cheryl smiled. "Then all I need is a patient."

"Your turn will come soon enough, Cheryl," Mitch said knowingly, his eyes turning back to the window, his brow creasing as he looked outside. "And when it does…" His voice trailed off, and Cheryl found herself frowning, too. She had only met Mitch Kannon a few hours ago, but something in his stance, his voice, told her there was more on his mind.

"What is it, Mitch?"

"Nothing."

He gave a brief shrug and flashed a smile Cheryl was sure was false. She just stared right back at him.

"I'm not going to fool you, am I."

"I know that look," Cheryl said, "and I know that voice, too. You're right Mitch. We're both in this game for a reason. So what's on your mind? What's worrying you?"

"I don't know." He shook his head. "The evacuation's going really well. The old school is filling up, more busloads are arriving from Corpus Christi as we speak, I've got extra staff in, just as requested—so why have I got…?"

He peered back out the window at the trees bending in the wind, the rain lashing so fiercely now that it didn't even make it to the ground, just hit the windows at right angles. Taking a deep breath, he moved his hand to his chest, rubbing it slowly, and for one awful moment Cheryl thought he was going to tell her he had chest pain. That Mitch Kannon, chief fire officer and lynch-pin of this whole evacuation plan, was having a heart attack. "I'm not going to keel over and die on you," Mitch said, seeing her worried expression.

"I wouldn't let you die," Cheryl assured him. "I'm all stocked up and ready to go, bar a couple of IV poles. Still, I have to admit I don't much fancy working that radio you were showing us earlier." Her voice grew more serious. "What is it, Mitch?"

"Have you ever been in a hurricane, Cheryl?"

She shook her head. "No, and I don't think I want to be. If it's like this here where people are being evacuated to, I can't imagine how bad it must be in Corpus Christi…." Her voice trailed off. "You don't think Hurricane Damon's going to hit here, do you? Is that what's worrying you?"

She waited for a reassuring smile, a dismissive flick of his hand, but Mitch just stared right back.

"But surely the weather bureau would know," Cheryl protested.

"We're dealing with Mother Nature here," Mitch told her. "And even with the brightest brains, the best equipment, the latest scientific techniques, there are no guarantees as to what she's got up her sleeve."

"But it can't hit here." Cheryl's voice was barely a whisper, her brain reeling at the possible consequences. "It just can't. Everyone's been moved to Turning Point to get *away* from the storm. If it comes here, if it hits the school…" Turning her head, she eyed the triage area she had set up. She had anticipated casualties coming in, and till now had felt prepared for any eventuality. But if the storm changed track and descended on Turning Point, then in a matter of hours this area would resemble a war zone—

"I could be wrong." Mitch broke in to her thoughts. "The experts all think I am."

"You've told them?" Cheryl asked. "You've told them your concerns?"

"For all the good it did."

She could hear the bitter note in his voice.

"I've lived here all my life. I know the land like the back of my hand, the shifts in the weather, the signs anyone who didn't know the place would miss—but will those folks at the weather bureau listen to me?" He shook his head. "Look, Cheryl, it's just a gut feeling at this stage, and I hope to God that I am wrong, but I have to admit I'm starting to get worried."

"So am I, then." Cheryl might have known Mitch Kannon for only a few hours, but she'd been around emergency personnel long enough to recognize that he wasn't the type to make a fuss unnecessarily. Mitch would have seen enough drama in his time without needing to invent it. "If you're right— I mean, if the storm does change course and end up hitting Turning Point, what will we do?" She gave a low laugh that to nonemergency personnel would have seemed out of place, but a dash of black humor was par for the course in this line of work. "Is there a plan B you haven't told us about?"

"Plan B's the same in Texas as it is in California, Cheryl. We just get on and deal with it." Mitch gave a rueful smile. "That's what we do best, isn't it? Deal with the chaos life throws up every now and then, pick up the pieces no one was expecting to fall."

Cheryl nodded grimly, already thinking ahead. "We'll need more blankets. I know they're setting up hot drinks and sandwiches at the school hall, the casualties that arrive here with their families might be cold and shocked. Can somebody organize extra coffee urns, soup…"

"I'll get straight on it."

Cheryl nodded gratefully. "And tell whoever you send in to Dr. Holland's room to grab whatever else they can, I'd rather have too much than too little. I'd better get back to stocking up now."

"You do that." Mitch nodded, and as a fire truck pulled into the station, he replaced the cap on his thermos. "I'd better go see what's up. It's good to have you on board, Cheryl."

"It's good to be here."

She set to work with renewed enthusiasm now. The triage area had been prepared to her liking. IV cannulas and swabs in kidney dishes, flasks of fluid hanging ready, neck collars, bandages, padding—everything was arranged to Cheryl's liking, but Mitch's ominous words had hit a note. Cheryl ran a couple of IVs through the lines so they would be ready as soon as a cannula was inserted into the patient. If the number of casualties was going to increase beyond her initial prediction, time would be of the essence. Cheryl knew she'd be grateful later for every second spent preparing for the victims now.

"I'VE GOT TWO GUYS heading over to Doc Holland's office." Mitch was back, running an approving eye over Cheryl's emergency area. "How are you doing?"

"Good. Everything's ready," Cheryl reported. "There's really not much more I can do here until patients start to arrive. This area's for the seriously injured. I've got all the emergency resuscitation equipment set up here. The walking wounded will have to wait over there till Amy or I can get to them." She gestured to the benches that lined the walls. "And anyone else will just have to wait their turn over at the school."

"Texans are a pretty uncomplaining lot. You don't have to worry about people lining up for a bandage they don't need. It shouldn't be too hard to keep this area for more serious cases."

"They build them tough here, then?" Cheryl smiled.

"Yep, they're a tough old lot. More worried about others than themselves. Which is why, if everything's set up, I'm going to have to pull you away from here for now."

"Pull away." Cheryl grinned, eager to get out in the field and finally do what she was trained for.

"Hal, one of my young firefighters, is trying to keep his mind on the job, but he's got a wife and five-day-old baby at home. They live a few miles out of Turning Point."

"Poor guy," Cheryl murmured. "No doubt he's worried how they're coping."

"Not only that," Mitch continued, "they've got a seven year old, as well, and apparently he's fallen over and hurt his arm. Beth, Hal's wife, reckons that the arm could be broken. That's why she called Hal, to see what she should do. The roads are too bad to be driving with a sick child and a new baby, but the little guy's in too much pain just to be left. Now, a firefighter with his mind wandering is the last thing I need today. If I can tell Hal that you're going out to check on them, it would put his mind at rest. I've called the weather bureau again, and they're still adamant I've got nothing to worry about. And even if my hunch is right, by all reports, nothing much is going to go down for a few hours yet."

"I'd be happy to go," Cheryl assured him, already packing her backpack with the equipment she would need to deal with the little boy's arm as Mitch gave her directions and a map. "I might as well see a bit of Texas while I'm here."

"Well, no stopping to get postcards," Mitch laughed, carrying on the joke. "I want you straight back here." He handed her a massive navy waterproof jacket, which Cheryl accepted gratefully. "All the fire vehicles are in use," he told her as they ventured outside.

The rain lashed at her cheeks, the wind catching in her throat, and it took an effort just to walk the short distance to the large dark Jeep parked across the street at the side of the fire station.

"You can use this," Mitch shouted, wrenching open the door and none-too gently pushing Cheryl inside.

"Whose is it?" Cheryl asked.

"It's my personal vehicle." Leaning over he pulled open the glove compartment to reveal a large stash of candy. "Help yourself, but save me a few."

She fiddled with the controls for a moment, checking the gears and the wipers.

"That's the demister," Mitch pointed out, unwrapping a candy and popping it into his mouth. "I reckon you'll be needing it, and you'd better get some gas, too," he added, looking at the gauge. "There's a station just down the road." Reaching into his pocket, he pulled out some bills and handed them to Cheryl.

"Is gas more expensive in Texas?" Cheryl asked with a wry smile. Mitch had given her enough cash to fill the jeep ten times over.

"Nope." Mitch grinned. "But I've just realized that we're low on one essential—chocolate."

"*Very* essential," Cheryl agreed.

"Get as much as you can when you get the gas, Cheryl. I admit to having a sweet tooth, but it's also a great pick-me-up for the crews."

"And a good bribery tool for the kids," Cheryl added. "I'll keep a bar in my pocket for my house call."

"You're sure you don't mind doing this on your own?" Mitch said. "If I could spare anyone, I'd send them out with you. I don't really like the idea of you out there on your…"

"I can read a map, Mitch." Starting the engine, she waited as Mitch stepped back. Then, after taking a final moment to familiarize herself with the controls, she waved to the fire chief and drove off into the lashing rain.

She found the gas station easily. Jumping down, Cheryl huddled inside the waterproof jacket. Mitch had been right. Her hospital scrubs and flimsy linen jacket would have been less than useless in these conditions. Dashing across the pavement, she ran into the small shop, groaning inwardly when she saw the lineup. Everyone was clearly out on a last-minute spree, stocking up on batteries and flashlights. Cheryl grabbed the last basket, filling it with chocolates before joining the line to pay. Just for the hell of it, she reached over and picked up a couple of postcards.

CHAPTER TWO

"SETTLE DOWN, GUYS." Noah Arkin shouted above the stamping feet and whinnying coming from the back of his van. "Just the gas to get, then only one more stop at the fire station and we can finally head for home."

His words had no effect, but then Noah hadn't really expected them to. Still, it didn't stop him from trying. The truck was jammed with medical equipment, cages and animals. He'd only gone out to drop supplies off to Mitch and should have been back at his clinic ages ago, but as usual, he'd been delayed. No way could he drive by his patients' homes without checking that they and their owners were okay. Of course he'd ended up battening down hatches and offering to evacuate people's pets to his clinic so their owners would have one less thing to worry about during the storm.

The last two days had been hell. Sure, farmers knew how best to prepare for a storm. They'd been through it often enough, after all, and this was their livelihood they were protecting, but there was still a lot of work for Noah: updating immunizations, helping ranchers move cattle to safer pastures. Unlike Mitch, who was dealing with the two-legged specimens, once the storm really took hold, Noah could sleep—crash in the little studio apartment attached to his clinic and catch up on some rest before the real work started. The worst time for veterinarians came after the storm. Apart from the inevitable casualties and missing animals, the power lines would be down and the water levels up, hindering rescue efforts.

But instead of being at home, Noah thought, stifling a yawn then raking a hand through his damp brown hair, instead of catching up on some rest, he still had the supplies to drop off and a van full of pets to sort out.

He had to toughen up.

Filling up the truck at the main station in town, Noah listened as the animals kicked at the side of his vehicle, the howls and barks growing louder now. As if he didn't have enough to do already without taking this bunch on. As if he didn't have enough to organize without acting as an unpaid baby-sitter for half of Turning Point's pets. And it would be unpaid, Noah knew that for sure. But the money side didn't worry him. His ranching clients provided his real bread-and-butter. The pets that had found their way into the back of his van were the jam on top.

Literally!

After the storm passed, he'd have umpteen more jars of jam to line his already heaving cupboards and enough farm eggs to start his own store.

No, it wasn't money that was the problem, it was time.

Over and over, that very precious commodity seemed to slip away from him. But how could he say no to Mrs.

Gessop when she asked him to look after her budgerigar, and how could he tell Old Mary that her beloved, over-weight and extremely spoilt miniature horse Georgina was the very last thing he needed to deal with right now?

He couldn't.

Schmuck! That should be his middle name. Pulling the nozzle out, Noah replaced the gas cap before running into the shop.

Noah Schmuck Arkin.

Jeez, Noah thought, looking at the long lineup in the store, he'd be in here for ages.

He eyed the basket of the customer in front of him, then did a double take. The basket was almost bursting with every type of chocolate and candy bar available. Someone clearly didn't believe in rationing! And the woman was idly reading postcards as if she had all the time in the world. But there was something else about her that caught Noah's attention. Something that made her stand apart from the rest of the people in the lineup. A certain aloofness that held him entranced.

She was tall, too.

Okay, Noah admitted, he liked tall women, and since he was six foot four himself, it wasn't hard to see why. But it wasn't just her height that made her stand out. It wasn't even the appalling baggy clothes she wore. Something told him that under that hideous jacket was a well-toned body. She carried herself regally, her back as straight as a ballet dancer's. And even though her long dark hair was pulled back in a ponytail, the lush heavy locks, wet from the rain, were straining to escape.

His eyes flicked down to her hands. They were well-groomed, he noted, the nails neat, not too long, an immaculate French polish the perfect touch.

She was, quite simply, beautiful.

"Just the gas, Noah?" Bill asked, seeing the bulging basket of the mystery woman, who was now at the counter, and rudely shouting over her.

Normally Noah would have shaken his head, said something along the lines of "No rush, Bill. Go ahead and serve the lady first."

And she certainly was a lady, Noah decided as she turned her head and he got a glimpse of velvety brown eyes framed with dark lashes, full dark lips pursing in indignation as he stepped forward to pay. Noah felt his heart skip into overdrive, his brain processing a million details in an instant. Take away the working man's clothes, take away the heavy boots, and underneath he knew, just knew, she was all woman.

All woman, a certain piece of his anatomy confirmed. But even if she was the most gorgeous woman to hit Turning Point in as long as he could remember, even if Bill's offer to serve him first could throw him an opening line here, Mother Nature was the only woman who could be on Noah's mind today.

He needed to out of here.

"Thanks, Bill," Noah said, handing over his money. "Thanks," he repeated to the woman, giving her an apologetic smile. And he waited—waited for a shrug, a wide Texas smile and an easy "No problem." Instead she was frowning, two vertical lines forming on the bridge of a deliciously snubbed nose. "I'm the local vet," he offered by way of explanation, but her frown only deepened.

"Gotta look after the animals," Bill chimed in, handing over Noah's change. "Especially with the storm coming."

"Oh, sure!" Chocolate Girl bristled. "Don't mind me."

Even Bill started at her confident New York accent and almost menacing velvet eyes. "I'm only here to look out for the humans."

Geesh!

Looks *and* attitude.

For a second, Noah found himself intrigued. He wanted to prolong the conversation, to see those angry lips move again, to catch another glimpse of those delicious eyes and find out just what this woman was doing in Turning Point. A reporter perhaps? Yeah, that seemed to fit. There were always reporters sniffing around for a story in a crisis. They'd be focusing on the *human* aspect of the storm, filling a lull in the hard news with some sixty-second human interest story. Noah could certainly picture the camera loving this woman.

But as stunning as she might be, Noah wasn't about to be spoken down to. "Hey, thanks for being so understanding," he shot back as he took his change from Bill. Even though his sarcasm was delivered with a wide smile, her frown deepened and he knew he'd ruffled her feathers.

"I'm not," she bristled, turning around to face him full-on.

If the side view had held Noah entranced, looking directly into her face took his breath away.

She was gorgeous.

Seriously so.

"I know you're not," Noah replied in a clipped tone. As gorgeous as she was, her stern gaze had him recovering quickly, and despite his earlier interest, Noah changed his mind. Even if time had allowed, he had no desire to have to justify his work to some uptight city babe who simply didn't get it— The ringing of his cell phone saved him from thinking up a smart reply, and he chose to move to the relative quiet of the back of the store as Bill unloaded Chocolate Girl's basket.

"Calm down, Jack." Noah's firm voice had the whole store turning to look at him. "No, stay the hell out of the stable. You'll get yourself killed if you go in while he's like that. I need you to calm down and tell me just how badly injured he is…."

Everything moved in slow motion for a moment, Bill's hands running up the total on the till, his eyes trained on Noah, the locals in the lineup holding their breath and hoping that somehow they'd got it wrong, that somehow they were misinterpreting the one-sided conversation. Jack and Sara had pooled everything on the prize stallion, a shining light in their tough times. He couldn't be going crazy in a stable on the other side of town, badly injured.

"I'll come now…." Noah said, trying to calm Jack down, to keep the note of fear out of his own voice. And it was genuine fear. A brute of an animal deranged with terror in a confined space wasn't the ideal combination. His voice trailed off as Jack made his decision, the toughest of calls, and handed the phone over to his wife.

The stallion might be a brute of an animal, but its legs were as fragile as glass, and from Jack's description, the fracture he had sustained was beyond repair.

Closing his eyes, blocking out the watching audience, Noah listened intently, his voice softer when he spoke next. "I'm right here, Sara. You just make sure Jack's safe in there…."

There was a long pause. And even though no one in the store heard the shot, everyone knew what had happened. Running a hand over his forehead, Noah spoke again, his voice deep, calm and reassuring.

"I'm sorry, buddy, really sorry. And I know it won't help now, but you know that you did the right thing."

Maybe he was out of line, but at that moment Noah was hurting. He wanted to lash out at someone, and it was Chocolate Girl's eyes that met his as he snapped the phone closed and replaced it in his pocket.

"Oh, well." He gave a shrug. "I guess it was only a horse."

MAYBE HE'D BEEN too harsh.

Okay, Noah conceded as he leaned against the truck and took a few deep breaths, he *had* been harsh. It wasn't her fault if she didn't understand how much animals really mattered here in Turning Point. He'd had no right to imply she didn't give a damn.

She probably didn't, though, Noah thought, but without malice now. How could anyone, unless they lived on the land, understand the delicate balance between man and beast; contemplate that without the animals,

Turning Point would be a virtual ghost town. Sure, there was agriculture, acre after acre of rich soil providing vital crops, but the animals were the beat of the land.

Climbing into his van, he started the engine, watching as the woman ran across the pavement, her long limbs breaking into an effortless sprint as if she were some beautiful thoroughbred. Her long dark ponytail streaming behind her, she held the plastic bags to her chest as if they contained some sort of treasure, and Noah held back the sudden urge to climb out and run over to her, to apologize for his behavior. But what would be the point? he reasoned, pulling away from the pumps and signaling right, glancing in his rearview mirror and seeing her blinker indicating left. No doubt she'd forgotten the whole incident by now and was driving off to wherever the action was, off to report on other people's misery….

"Hey, Madge." He smiled as his faithful old dog nuzzled at his hand for a stroke. Dark eyes stared back at him—endearing eyes, but not nearly as endearing as the woman who had just breezed in and out of his life and whirled up a ministorm of her own. His cell phone was ringing again and Noah forcibly pushed the image of Chocolate Girl out of his mind; he had enough to be getting on with today without daydreaming about some woman he'd barely said two words to. That thought was further confirmed as he put the call on to Speaker, frowning as the anxious voice of another usually laid-back farmer filled the van, intermittent bleeps indicating that yet another caller was trying to get through….

And a feeling that had been creeping up for a couple of hours now took hold of Noah. Gripping the steering wheel as he drove into town, he wished he possessed some sort of virtual dream catcher, something that could trap the uneasy thoughts that were flooding his mind now, quash the fears that were starting to take hold....

...halt an approaching nightmare.

"HEY, NOAH!" Mitch Kannon came running over as Noah started to unload the equipment. "Been picking up a few strays on your travels?"

"I wish." Noah shrugged, but his moment of self-pity was wasted on Mitch Kannon. The fire chief would be in no mood to hear about some stranger Noah had *almost* met in a gas station. A stranger who Noah simply couldn't quite manage to push out of his thoughts. There was something about her that had him enthralled, something about her elusiveness that served to drag him in. Sure, she hadn't exactly been endearing, hadn't exactly bowled him over with her charm. And yet...

"Is business so bad that you need to pick up strays?" Mitch asked with a grin.

"I'm driving with blinkers on from now on," Noah admitted. "Strays are the last thing I need right now."

"Trouble?" Mitch asked perceptively, helping Noah unload the van and carry the equipment into the building.

"I took a call from Jack Sawyer half an hour ago."

"And?"

"Had to listen as he put a bullet through Blaze...."

"What?" Mitch shook his head, genuinely appalled at the news.

"There was nothing I could do—he'd gone crazy, taken fright and fractured his leg. It was a severe fracture. Even if I'd been there, I don't doubt for a second that the outcome would have been the same. Jack had no choice. It was the humane thing to do. Must have hurt like hell, though," he added as they headed back to the van, unloading the last of the supplies. The animals caged in the back made frantic noises.

"They're pretty worked up," Mitch commented as a loud *thud* sounded against the side of the van, causing the fire chief to jump.

"You should try driving with them," Noah said, heaving the last of the supplies out of the truck and following Mitch back to the station. "Either it's the mother of all storms about to hit Corpus Christi, or the predictions are wrong and it's heading this way!"

It had been a joke—sort of.

Mitch set the large box he carried down onto the floor inside the station. Noah did the same.

"You're well set up," Noah said, staring around the room.

"It wasn't me." Mitch shrugged. "The team from California are efficient to say the least, and believe me, right now, I'm more than happy that I sent for reinforcements when I did." He took a deep breath. "What makes you think the storm could be heading this way, Noah?" Mitch's voice was serious, his question delivered in his usual direct way with not a hint of scorn attached, which told Noah his concerns were being taken seriously.

"The animals are going crazy," Noah said. "I know that's not much to go on. I mean, they always get upset by storms, and I'm used to them acting weird at times for no reason, but you should hear them back at the clinic, Mitch. They're climbing the cages, pacing like crazy. Look at what's just happened to Blaze, and it's not only him. I've had a couple more farmers calling to tell me the animals are starting to panic. They're acting just as they did last time a big storm headed this way."

"It's *not* heading this way, though." Mitch shook his head.

His voice was firm, but something in his eyes told Noah that the chief didn't believe his own words.

"I've just been on to the weather bureau, and they're still convinced it's heading for Corpus Christi."

"*Still* convinced? So you've already been on to the bureau and told them that you're worried." When Mitch didn't answer, Noah persisted. "Which means you're thinking along the same lines as me, doesn't it."

"Yep."

"Damn, we've got the school filling with evacuees from Corpus Christi, we've got busloads still heading in…."

"And my daughter's out there."

Mitch never played the emotion card, and seeing the chief's worried eyes, Noah felt as if he had been hit in the chest with an iron fist.

"What do you want me to do, Mitch?" Noah respected Mitch, and if there was anything he could do to help, then Noah would do it. "Do you want me to call the bureau, tell them how the animals are reacting?"

He half expected Mitch to laugh, to tell him that the bureau wasn't about to listen to some veterinarian with a half-baked idea that his animals were talking to him, but when Mitch gave a worried nod, Noah's heart sank.

"It's worth a try."

It took forever for Noah to get through. No doubt half of Turning Point was trying to contact the bureau, as well. These people knew their land, knew the shifts in the weather. They'd been through enough hurricanes and floods to know when trouble was in the air, and it was in the air now, Noah could feel it. The rain was pelting down and the wind howled angrily; even inside the fire station Noah was forced to shout into the phone just to be heard.

"What did they say?" Mitch asked as Noah replaced the receiver in its cradle.

"That by their calculations we've got nothing to worry about. That we're to carry on with the evacuation protocol as outlined."

"Damn!" Mitch banged his fist down on the desk in exasperation. "We're like sitting ducks. The storm's getting worse by the minute, I've got teams out there doing rescues. I've even had an emergency team flown *in* to the area, when I should have been getting everyone the hell out. I've sent them on rescues—"

"You didn't know at the time the storm was heading

this way," Noah said. "We still don't know for sure, Mitch." Taking a couple of breaths, he willed himself to stay calm. There was no point losing their heads. "We still don't," Noah said again, but more firmly this time, and Mitch nodded back, his face taut with tension but back in full control now.

"Noah, I know your animals mean everything to you. And I know that at times like this you're supposed to be at the clinic…."

"They're not humans, Mitch." Noah knew what was coming. He loved his animals and his old house that was attached to the sparkling modern clinic he had built from the ground up. The veterinary clinic was his life. Every waking moment of his day was filled with caring for animals. But he was highly skilled and trained in medical procedures, and if he and Mitch were right and the storm was heading this way, then Noah knew that his skills would be put to better use right here in town.

Saving human lives.

"I'm going back to the clinic, Mitch. I'll secure the animals that I've got in the van and make sure the rest are okay, then I'll lock up and come straight back to town."

"I hate to ask this of you, Noah."

"You didn't ask." Noah gave a wry smile. "I offered. Let's just hope I'm not needed. Let's just hope we're both worrying about nothing."

"Let's hope, huh?"

Noah was running toward the exit now, racing to get back to the clinic and tend to the animals so he could return to town and help. But something stopped him at the door, a feeling he couldn't identify.

"What's up, Noah?" Mitch asked, coming over to him.

Noah stood there, eyeing the rows of equipment all neatly set up, and the sense of foreboding that had niggled now, churned his stomach.

"If you didn't know the area, Mitch, didn't know just how bad the storms and floods can be here, what would you do?"

"Find out the hard way, I guess." Mitch started to joke, but when he realized Noah was serious, he changed tack. "There're announcements every few minutes on the radio, Noah. I've got teams out there guiding people to the evacuation centers. Even if you didn't know the area, you'd soon figure out what was coming and find somewhere safe."

"I guess so."

"What's on your mind, Noah?" Mitch asked.

"I don't know." Noah gave a shrug, embarrassed to find Mitch eying him with concern. How could he explain to this down-to-earth guy this strange fear that seemed to be clutching his heart?

It wasn't just his belief there was a storm heading this way that was making him feel so edgy. He thought of those velvet brown eyes that had held his for a moment in time.

Chocolate Girl was out there in a town that was turning more dangerous by the minute, and for reasons he couldn't rationalize even to himself, it terrified the hell out of him.

CHAPTER THREE

"I'M THE LOCAL VET!" Pulling a face, Cheryl did a pale imitation of Noah's voice as she drove angrily along. Even with a few miles safely between them, she was still stinging from the encounter at the gas station, still smarting from the *local vet's* remarks as well as her own part in the exchange. She wished she could hit the rewind button on that awful conversation. Why hadn't she just turned and said "No problem" when Dr. Perfect jumped the queue?

That was what normal people did. Cheryl sighed. That was exactly what her response would have been two years ago: she would have shrugged and given an easy smile, bitten her tongue over a minor annoyance, instead of charging like a bull at a red flag, provoking confrontation…erecting barriers.

It was almost second nature to her now, putting up protective screens around her heart the second she felt her guard was down. One look at the local vet and her guard had fallen around her ankles like a pair of panties without elastic. Good-looking, friendly and able to deflect her barbs—a heady combination, and the very last thing she needed right now. The very last thing she needed *full stop,* Cheryl thought, forcibly pushing all thoughts of the handsome stranger out of her mind. Pulling over to the side of the road, she checked her map. The directions and landmarks that had seemed so straightforward when Mitch had given them to her were almost useless now with the wipers going at full tilt and visibility down to near zero.

If the weather had been bad an hour ago, it was dire now.

She had to be near her destination, Cheryl reasoned, running a finger along the map, following her journey from Turning Point. There was the garage where she'd filled up the Jeep, there was the crossroad where she'd swung left, and over there... Wiping the side window with the sleeve of her coat, Cheryl glanced over at the swollen river gushing rapidly alongside the road, its dirty gray surf rolling more like waves on an ocean, before she turned back to the map. She'd followed the instructions to the letter, so where the hell was the farmhouse? She thought about calling Mitch, but decided to leave that as a last resort. Mitch didn't have time to hold her hand today. Maybe she could wave down a passing car. But knowing her luck, it would be that smug vet that stopped to help. His already overinflated ego would be pumped up a touch further when he saw the scrape she was in....

"Stop it," Cheryl scolded herself. Why was she allowing herself to dwell on something so irrelevant? Wiping down the windows again, she was about to reach for the phone and admit she was hopelessly lost, when a driveway she could have sworn hadn't been there a couple of moments ago appeared in her sideview mirror. Cheryl allowed herself a triumphant smile.

She'd made it on her own!

"THANK YOU SO MUCH for coming out to us."

As Beth ushered her into the hallway, the first thing to hit Cheryl was the delicious smell of home baking.

"You have no idea how much I appreciate this," Beth said. "I know how busy everyone is today."

"It is Beth, isn't it?" Cheryl asked, shaking the woman's hand briefly. "I'm Cheryl Tierney. Mitch told me you've got a little guy in a lot of pain who needs to be seen."

"I do. His name's Flynn."

"Flynn." Cheryl smiled at the small boy lying on the sofa as Beth showed her through to the living area. The smell of baking gave way to that delicious new-baby smell, the powdery, milky scent of innocence. Cheryl glanced over to the crib in the corner. A tiny precious bundle lay sleeping quietly there. She turned back to the boy. His arm was elevated on a cushion, his green eyes staring up at her, and for a tiny guilt-tinged moment, Cheryl felt something so alien it took a second to register. The feeling that seemed to reach out and knot her stomach in one single-handed motion was jealousy. If Cheryl had made a blueprint of her life ten years ago, this was where she would have liked to be at the ripe old age of thirty-one.

At home with her babies.

Not a visiting nurse, frozen to the core, hair plastered to her scalp. Not a newly divorced, slightly brittle career woman, with a fitness regime that would rival that of any sports professional. Okay, Turning Point wasn't exactly New York, and her ex-husband Joe was a lawyer rather than a firefighter, but the home Beth had created had Cheryl's throat tightening. Long suppressed dreams momentarily surfaced as she glimpsed the life she had thought she'd be leading, and she felt a pang of homesickness for a city she still missed and a family that had fallen apart.

Oh, she'd fallen in love with Courage Bay. She'd embraced the healthy outdoor lifestyle with open arms, joined a gym within a few weeks of arriving and shopped till she'd dropped on rather too many occasions. Fashion was a newly discovered passion of Cheryl's, now that her salary wasn't tied up in Joe's education. And she loved the challenges of her work as a trauma nurse at Courage Bay Hospital.

But as happy as she was, as fulfilled as her life might be, every now and then her loss hit her as if it had all happened only yesterday. Anything could set her off. An elderly couple walking hand in hand along the beach reminded her of her parents, a hotshot lawyer on a TV show resembled her ex-husband Joe, a baby sleeping in its pram recalled lost dreams. And now a seven-year-old boy named Flynn, with green eyes and blond hair….

"Hi, Flynn." Cheryl smiled at him, pushing her own feelings aside, remembering in an instant why she was here. "My name's Cheryl."

"Are you a doctor?" he asked in a lisping voice.

His two front teeth were missing, and his eyes were so suspicious Cheryl found herself smiling.

"No," she answered. "There wasn't a doctor free to come out, so I'm afraid you'll have to make do with me. I'm a trauma nurse."

"What's that?"

Cheryl didn't mind the questions a bit; at least they took Flynn's mind off his injury as she gently examined it. "Well, I work in the emergency department of a hospital in Courage Bay, California."

"So you see lots of injured people, then?" Flynn asked his eyes widening. "Do you see guts hanging out and legs falling off?"

"Flynn!" Beth broke in. "Where did you learn to speak like that?"

"Oh, that's okay." Cheryl winked at her small patient. "It's a perfectly good question. I see lots of things," Cheryl replied assuredly as she examined his arm, wincing inside as Flynn bit back a yelp. She decided to prolong the rather gory conversation just to keep Flynn's mind off his pain as she gently palpated the swollen wrist. "Lots of blood and guts, though I haven't seen too many legs falling off."

"Oh." Flynn gave a disappointed shrug. "Hanging off, then?"

"Hanging off?" Cheryl frowned, as if she was thinking hard. "Yep, now you mention it, I've seen a few of them."

"Sick!" Flynn exclaimed, and from his enthusiastic smile, Cheryl assumed that meant he was suitably impressed.

"Apparently *sick*'s the new word for *cool*." Beth sighed as Cheryl finished her examination and gently placed the boy's arm back onto the pillow. "Normally, I'd never worry Hal when he's out on call." She was ringing her hands in concern as she watched her son. "But Flynn's been in agony since he fell, though you wouldn't think it to look at him now. I gave him some painkillers, but if you'd seen him before…"

"The painkillers would have kicked in by now—and now he's not moving his arm and he's sitting quietly, which is why he's not upset. He had good reason to make a fuss and you had every reason to call your husband." Cheryl looked up at Beth. "He's broken his wrist."

"Sick!" Flynn shouted, as Beth promptly dissolved into tears.

"Now, how about you lie there quietly for a moment, Flynn, while I speak to your mom, and soon I'll be back and we can see about making your arm a bit more comfortable."

"I'm sorry," Beth gulped as they reached the kitchen. "I know it's only a broken wrist and you probably think I'm overreacting. It's just that…"

"It's the last thing you need right now," Cheryl said as Beth nodded slowly. "You've got a new baby, Beth. It's no wonder you're upset that Flynn's broken his arm. Any mother would be."

"I suppose." Beth didn't sound particularly convinced or comforted. "Do you have kids, Cheryl?"

"No." Cheryl gave a small smile. "But I've seen

enough moms in my line of work to know that your re-action to Flynn's injury is perfectly normal. There's nothing wrong with shedding a few tears."

"Oh, don't mind me." Beth forced a smile. "I'm fine. The kettle's just boiled, Cheryl. Can I make you a drink before you get started?"

"Not for me, thanks. I'd best get started on setting that wrist."

"Well, after then," Beth suggested. "I've made some cookies…."

But Cheryl shook her head, keen to get the job done and return to town.

"I think Mitch will want me to head straight back. If you can find me a bucket that would be great. I'll also need some warm water for the plaster and a few tow-els." Taking her cue, Beth scurried out of the kitchen, and Cheryl unloaded her backpack on the freshly scrubbed table. Come to think of it, everything was freshly scrubbed—the place was spotless.

Immaculate even.

So why didn't it sit right? Cheryl wondered.

"Are you going to put on a cast?" Beth asked, return-ing loaded with towels and a bucket.

Cheryl shook her head. "Just a temporary back slab, but that should be enough to provide some relief for Flynn. His wrist doesn't look displaced." As Beth frowned, Cheryl checked herself and spoke in layman's terms. "I'm pretty sure it's just a small break with no de-formity, but it will need to be confirmed by X ray. Given the weather, I think your chances of a trip to the hospital are slim. So for now, we'll stick with the back slab. First, I bandage the arm with cotton wool, then put on a slab of plaster of Paris, which I'll mold to his arm and attach with a bandage. It'll come off easily when he gets to the hospital, but that will give him a lot of support and take care of his pain till then. Just keep his wrist in a sling, and once the storm is over, you can take him for an X ray and no doubt they'll put on a more substantial cast."

"And he'll be fine," Beth said firmly, flashing a smile, but the sparkle of tears in her eyes didn't go unnoticed by Cheryl.

She narrowed her eyes in concern. Something told her that no matter how much she was needed back in Turning Point, for a moment or two she was needed here, as well.

"Is there anything else on your mind, Beth—apart from Flynn, I mean? Anything else worrying you?"

"Oh, you haven't got time to listen to my moans," Beth said airily. "Mitch will be wondering where you've got to."

"Mitch can wait awhile," Cheryl said gently. "Sometimes it helps to talk…."

"Oh, what would you know?" Beth's voice was brittle. "I suppose you think it's easy. I suppose you think that keeping house is child's play compared to what you do." Aghast, Beth clapped her hands to her mouth. "I'm sorry. I'm so sorry. You've been nothing but nice and I…"

"It's all right, Beth." Cheryl kept her voice calm.

Beth's words might have stung but they weren't aimed at her personally. Cheryl had been nursing long enough to know when someone was near the edge. Beth's defensiveness and passive-aggressive responses were signs that needed to be heeded before Cheryl left this vulnerable woman alone with two small children. Tears were flowing freely now, and in the absence of tissues, Beth wept into the towel she was holding, her shoulders heaving as she let out whatever it was she had been keeping in. Instinctively Cheryl headed around the table, dragging a chair over and sitting by Beth.

"I'm so sorry," Beth sobbed.

"Forget it," Cheryl said gently. "What's going on, Beth?"

"You haven't got time for this."

"That's for me to decide," Cheryl said firmly, taking the pressure off Beth while assuring her patient that she was in control. At the same time Cheryl was painfully aware that she didn't have the luxury of sitting for hours. It was up to Beth. If she needed help, then she had to reach out now.

"I'm so worried, I can't sleep, can't sit down."

Still Cheryl said nothing, just held the other woman's gaze.

"Hal says that I'm being stupid, that there's nothing wrong with Paul."

"The new baby?" When Beth nodded, Cheryl pushed further, feeling her way slowly, unsure of the real issue here but knowing that whatever it was, it was big to Beth. "So you've got two boys now," Cheryl probed.

She was careful not to offer congratulations, not to assume, as most people might, that this should make Beth happy. When the woman literally crumpled before her, Cheryl knew she had been right.

"It should have been three." Beth's voice was a pale whisper, and Cheryl held her breath, knowing that the instinctive murmur of sympathy on her lips was not what Beth needed right now. "I should have had three little boys, but my second son, Cody, died."

"How old was Cody?" Cheryl asked softly when it was clear Beth wasn't going to volunteer anything more. "When he died?"

"Eight weeks old." Beth pressed her fingers into her eyes, taking a few gulping breaths before continuing. "Sudden Infant Death Syndrome. I put him down for his afternoon sleep in his room...." She shook her head fiercely, clearly not ready to relive the experience, yet desperately needing to talk. "Hal was out on the farm with Noah...."

"Noah?" Cheryl asked, the name familiar, answering her own question in her mind before Beth did.

"He's Turning Point's veterinarian."

And local hero, to boot, Cheryl thought with a dash of bitterness as she recalled their encounter at the gas station. But Noah wasn't the issue here, Beth was, and Cheryl listened intently.

"They heard me screaming and came straight in. Poor Flynn. He saw everything. He still remembers it. He has nightmares about it every now and then." She gave a loaded sigh. "We all do."

"I'm so sorry." Her expression of sympathy was appropriate now, and Cheryl squeezed Beth's hand to show it was heartfelt.

"The coroner said everything that could have been done, had been. Hal and Noah were amazing. He even said that if there had been a hospital next door, they couldn't have done anything more for Cody."

"Did that help?"

"Not at the time," Beth admitted, "but it does a bit now, especially since we've got Paul. At least now I know that there was nothing we could have done to prevent Cody's death. Everything possible was done to try to save him. But when it happened, I was beyond consoling. I fell to pieces for a while."

"Which is understandable. How about Hal?"

"He was devastated, of course, but in a different way. He'd take himself off to the farm or out to the toolshed out back for hours on end, fixing things up, building things we didn't need. He just wouldn't talk about it to me."

"Men generally deal with grief in a different way, Beth. They tend to keep it in, whereas women like to talk."

"Don't we." A watery smile trembled on her lips. "He didn't want me to have another baby. He wasn't sure I'd be able to cope, and it seems he was right. I can't sleep, I can't let Paul out of my sight, and now poor Flynn's gone and broken his arm because I wasn't watching him properly because I was too scared to leave Paul."

Beth's tears were starting again, and hating herself for her insensitivity, Cheryl sneaked a quick look at her watch.

"He's a seven-year-old boy," she said firmly. "And seven-year-old boys are notorious for breaking bones. Believe me, I see it every day. You need support, Beth." Cheryl squeezed the other woman's hand again. "Everything you've told me—how you're feeling, Hal's reaction, your fears for the new baby—are completely normal reactions, given what you've been through. Is there anyone here you can talk to?"

"I've got lots of friends." Beth shrugged. "My mom's nearby." But her expression belied her positive words and she started to cry again. "They just don't understand, though. Dr. Holland was great. He warned me I'd feel like this. He said he'd call in, and that I could phone him anytime day or night if I was feeling anxious."

"He sounds nice," Cheryl ventured. "He's the one who just had the heart attack, isn't he?"

Beth nodded. "He's Turning Point's one and only doctor, but he was more than a doctor to me, he was a friend. Noah's good—the vet," she added, and Cheryl nodded. "He comes round for a drink every now and then and lets me ramble on about Cody and that horrible day, but I know, even if he tries not to show it, that he's not really into babies. Not the two-legged type anyway. He's only interested in his career."

"I know the type," Cheryl said, deliberately keeping the edge from her voice. But she did know the type—she'd been married to one, after all.

"There's no one I can really talk to about it, Cheryl. No one at all."

Only then did Beth's plight really hit Cheryl. God, how she wished she were at work. Piles of leaflets and phone numbers were available at the nurses' station. A psychiatrist was just a telephone call away.

But there weren't such resources here, and even her time was in short supply.

"Beth, if there was any way I could put things off I'd stay awhile longer, but I really do have to get back." Cheryl squeezed her hand again. "I have to set Flynn's arm and return to town, but please don't think I'm just walking out on you. You really do need some help, and I'm going to do my best to see you get it. Do you want me to ask Mitch to send Hal home?"

Immediately Beth shook her head.

"Please, Cheryl, don't. It will only make things worse. Look, I'm not about to do anything stupid. I just need some help."

"Well, you've taken the most difficult step—admitting it," Cheryl said softly.

"If I could just get a decent night's sleep—"

"You need a bit more than that," Cheryl broke in. "But it would be a good start. Look…" Standing up, Cheryl turned on a smile and hit Beth with a good dose of practical assertion. "I'm going to speak to Amy Sherwood about you. She's a doctor who's come to Turning Point to help with the evacuation. Now, I'm not going to lie and say she's going to race over. We're supposed to be here to deal with an emergency…." Cheryl's voice trailed off as she realized her insensitivity. Okay, this wasn't exactly the cutting edge of trauma nursing, but it *was* an emergency to this family at least, and as a nurse, as a woman, Cheryl knew that she couldn't just dismiss this family's problems, and neither would Amy. "She's a great doctor, and once I've explained your situation to her, I know that she'll want to help. Of course, we'll first have to see how the storm pans out, but once it's over, either you can come into town or Amy will come out to you before we head back to Courage Bay. We can get the ball rolling. Look, if you ask her nicely, she might even throw in a prescription for something to help you sleep." That comment lightened the loaded atmosphere just enough for Cheryl to do the hard bit.

"I really do have to get back, Beth. I'm sorry I haven't got more time…."

"I understand." Beth nodded bravely, and Cheryl's heart went out to her, every shred of nursing instinct telling her that this woman really needed help.

For the next little while Flynn was a model patient, asking endless questions as Cheryl applied the back slab. An incredulous smile broke out on his face as Cheryl bandaged over the plaster slab.

"It doesn't hurt anymore," he said.

"Great, isn't it?" Cheryl grinned. "But keep it dry, or it will go all soggy."

"Thanks so much again," Beth said as she followed Cheryl to the hallway. "For everything, Cheryl."

"Can Flynn have this?" Pulling a chocolate bar out of her pocket, Cheryl gave it to Beth who seemed to remember something and dashed off.

"Wait there!" she called, but was back seconds later

with a large tin. "The cookies I baked." She smiled, handing them over. "Share them around the crews, but make sure Hal gets a couple from me."

"Will do, on one condition."

"What's that?"

"You get back inside and put your feet up. Forget the housework, forget the baking, concentrate on you and your boys for now."

CHERYL WOULD HAVE RUN to the Jeep, but the wind was so strong, it was more a case of two steps forward, one step back. And as for breathing… Cheryl had no trouble getting air in. It whipped into her throat and pushed its way into her lungs uninvited—but breathing out was almost impossible. The driver door swung back in her hands as she opened it, and she had to battle the wind to close it once she was inside.

Starting the engine, Cheryl prepared to drive off. The rain was so loud on the roof, she at first didn't register the pounding on the driver's window, then frowned in concern as she saw a drenched Beth banging furiously on it.

Cheryl didn't dare try opening the door again. Pushing the power window switch, she felt a moment's unease, wondering what on earth could have forced Beth to leave her son and baby and run out in this weather.

"What's happened?"

"The storm's shifting course," Beth shouted against the wind. "It just came over the radio…."

Cheryl felt her heart lurch. Mitch had been right!

"Is it going to hit Turning Point?"

"They're not sure, but it's swerved from its predicted course and it's coming closer than they expected. A couple of nearby rivers have already burst their banks. You need to get back, and quickly, before the route back to town floods and you're stuck here!"

Cheryl nodded. "Get inside, Beth." The wind almost whipped the words out of her mouth. "Secure the house."

"I will." Beth nodded. "There's a shortcut you could take." She was pointing behind the house. "There's a private road. Follow it down, then take a left at Hansen's Barn."

"Where?"

"Hansen's Barn. You won't be able to miss it. It's an old, derelict barn. There's a bridge…"

The conversation was becoming more difficult with every word, and Cheryl shouted over the wind. "The road behind your house?"

Beth gave a rapid nod. "Then swing a left."

"Call Mitch," Cheryl instructed her. "Tell him I'm coming. And Beth…get inside!"

Cheryl could feel the adrenaline kick in as she drove off, only this time it wasn't welcome. It wasn't the usual surge of excitement that hit her when an alert came in. This was the first fluttering of real panic as she contemplated what they could be facing if Hurricane Damon hit this region full force. She thought of her colleagues, Dana, Nate and Amy, all out on calls.

Would they know?

Stay calm, Cheryl. The mantra pounded in her head, She had to get back to town. Once there, she'd have the answers. She'd be in a position to do something. She'd be back in control—

"Hell!" The curse slipped out of her lips as a dark bundle dashed across the road, too quickly for Cheryl to swerve. She slammed on the brakes, skidding to a halt just in time to avoid hitting the object.

Craning her neck, she peered out at the roadside, her heart rate slowly returning to its already accelerated state. A fox perhaps, running for shelter. Immediately she wished she hadn't checked the rearview mirror and caught a glimpse of solemn eyes and a shivering mass of fur. If only she were one of those people who could just drive right on.

But she wasn't.

Cheryl pulled up her collar and forced the door open. She had no desire to venture outside again into the driving wind and rain, but she had no choice now that she knew it was a dog.

"Come on, little guy." She crouched by her vehicle. "You're not looking at some sentimental animal lover here. This lady's in a rush, so if you want a ride, this is your only chance."

What was she doing? A category four hurricane was about to hit, and here she was, trying to coax a stupid dumb mutt into the van. What was Mitch's reaction going to be when she arrived back at the station with an extra passenger?

"Last chance," she warned, shaking her head in exasperation when the little dog refused to move. She had to walk away and head back to town. But as she climbed inside the Jeep, the smell of Beth's fresh-baked cookies was the first thing to hit her.

"Very last chance," Cheryl corrected wryly, stepping back down from the Jeep and holding out a cookie, which was fast dissolving in the rain, to the shivering mutt. "Come on, little guy."

It wasn't going to work, and even though Cheryl wasn't the world's greatest animal lover, it tore at her heart to turn her back. But a lost black dog must surely be way down on her list of priorities.

He might not be lost, Cheryl consoled herself as she resumed what was becoming a familiar struggle to close the car door. He was probably hotfooting his way back to his home right now. But suddenly, with an indignant yelp, a wedge of wet fur clambered furiously onto Cheryl's lap, then whining in protest as she pushed him over to the passenger seat. He agreed to stay put only when Cheryl placed a pile of Beth's cookies on the seat beside her.

"Somehow, I don't think you were heading for home, little guy," she said sadly, feeling the skinny ribs under the matted black fur. But there was no time for sympathy now. Slipping the emergency brake off, Cheryl glanced over at her companion, who was munching away, looking up every now and then with grateful eyes.

"What shall we call you, huh? You need a name." He was chomping away with gusto, somehow whimpering with delight at the same time. "Buster," Cheryl said out loud. "We'll call you Buster." The dog looked up for a second and met her eyes. "Hey, Buster, save a couple of cookies for Hal." Cheryl grinned as she drove on. "Or Beth will never forgive me."

There was the barn, just as Beth had said.

Letting out a sigh of relief, Cheryl peered over the flat landscape at the massive, deserted barn Beth had assured her she couldn't miss.

"Where to now, huh?" Despite the demister, the windows were steaming up at an alarming rate. She wiped the windshield with the back of her hand and drove slowly, visibility decreasing with every slow lurch forward.

She'd have to call Mitch and tell him she was lost. As if that wasn't just what the guy needed right now! But Mitch must have been thinking along the same lines, because before she'd even pulled out the cell phone he had given her, it rang shrilly in her hand.

There's a bridge. Beth's instructions played over in her mind as Cheryl pressed the answer button. There was a bridge, but not for much longer, Cheryl thought darkly, watching the swollen river rising, torrents of water sweeping along the banks, huge branches circling like tiny twigs as the current swept them along.

Pressing the phone to her ear, she braced herself for a few sharp words from the fire chief.

"Where the hell…" He got no further before his voice broke up.

Cheryl shouted back, not sure whether he could hear. "I'm five minutes away, Mitch. Beth told me that the storm's heading this way!" She was at the edge of the river now, and pulled open the glove compartment. Finding a rag inside, she took a moment to wipe the windshield clear. "She told me a shortcut. I'm at Hansen's Barn. I'm just coming over the bridge, so I should be with you soon." Although she strained to hear, there was only a crackling noise, broken by occasional fragments of Mitch's words.

"I won't be much longer, Mitch!" Cheryl shouted. "I can't hear you, you're breaking up. I'll be back soon." Putting the phone down, intending to resume the conversation once she was safely across the river, Cheryl edged the vehicle forward, her nose practically against the windshield now as she strained to see. She chewed her lip nervously as she eyed the rickety bridge. From what Cheryl could make out, the wooden structure looked about as stable as old Hansen's Barn.

But surely Beth would know, Cheryl reasoned. She was a local, for goodness' sake, and already her directions had cut Cheryl's journey in half.

The windshield wipers might just as well have been off now. The river was rising with each passing moment and Cheryl's mind flicked back to the triage area she'd set up at the station. Victims of the storm might already be there, injured and needing help.

Urging the vehicle slowly forward, she glanced over at her little friend. Trusting, wide eyes looked back at her. "Almost there," she said bravely, more for her own benefit than for Buster's. "Almost there," she said again. There was no thought of looking down. She was too damn busy concentrating on keeping the vehicle straight on the narrow bumpy bridge. As the Jeep lurched violently sideways, her first thought was a blown tire.

Terrified, she forced herself to look out the window and actually witnessed the side rails of the bridge snapping like taut string. Buster started barking in frenzied terror, and only then did the inevitability of what was about to happen finally register. Cheryl heard herself scream as the vehicle took a nosedive toward the water.

She'd expected to witness drama and excitement here in Turning Point, and inevitable casualties, but not for a second had it entered her head that today she might die.

CHAPTER FOUR

HE'D LEAVE THE RADIO ON.

Loud.

It was the only thing Noah could come up with, the only thing he could think of that might offer some comfort to the animals while he went back into town to help Mitch.

It was almost beyond his comprehension that he would be leaving them. These animals were so much more than his livelihood, so very much more than a job to him. But people came first, he knew that deep down. And today he had no choice.

But, Noah thought now as he drove toward the clinic, the radio announcer might start getting anxious, and any urgency in his voice would only worry the animals. Perhaps CDs instead?

Wiping the foggy windows with the back of his hand, he thought about all the jobs he had to get through when he finally made it home—locking up the animals, giving out some drugs, filling their water bottles and bowls, leaving out food. Yes, he'd stack some CDs on the portable player for them, a mixture of rock and dance, a couple of classical golden oldies for Georgina the miniature horse. He'd switch the CD player to batteries and leave it on low for them.

"Mabel!" He shouted the name out loud as it sprang into his head, sending the animals in the rear into a frenzy. But Madge didn't even turn a hair, more than used to her master's occasional eccentricity.

"She'll freak," Noah exclaimed, thinking of the massive pig in his shed due to farrow her first litter at any moment. "She's going to freak, Madge."

Madge raised one tired eye and Noah swore the old girl shook her head, reassuring him just as she always did.

They'd be fine.

"No!" This time his shout was instinctive, guttural, his body rigid with disbelief. Madge was immediately standing on the passenger seat and barking, her ears pricking up.

"No." The word strangled in his throat and his van skidded to an untidy halt as he slammed his foot down hard on the brake. His eyes widened in horror as the reality of what he was witnessing sank in.

Someone was on Hansen's Bridge.

On Hansen's Bridge, for God's sake!

No one went on Hansen's Bridge. It was derelict and had been closed off for as long as Noah could remember. There were Closed signs everywhere, a barrier even....

But in this weather, who could see them?

His eyes scanned the pounding water. The flimsy barrier wouldn't have stood a chance against its force, but the locals knew it was a death trap.

Only a fool or a stranger in town would be nudging

his vehicle along the bridge and hoping to make it over to the other side, but someone was doing just that! Inching his Jeep along the rickety bridge before Noah's disbelieving eyes.

His hands raked through his hair, gripping it for a moment as he shook his head in horror. His breathing was so rapid he had to tell himself forcibly to slow it down, but he never even finished the thought. Instead he jumped out of the van, roaring at the driver on the bridge to get back. Although as he gestured furiously, Noah knew it was useless. There was no way the Jeep was going to make it. Already he could see the wood buckling. Any minute now, the whole bridge would collapse like a pack of cards.

Think, Noah!

He raced around to the back of the van and wrenched the door open, shouting at the animals to stay back. Rummaging through the rope used to secure animals, he pulled out the longest before discarding the rest on the muddy ground beneath him. Slamming the door closed, he realized with a shock that he was already too late. A terrified female scream resonated in his skull as the bridge buckled farther and the vehicle lurched dangerously closer to the swirling water. He held his own scream in. He would need every last breath.

Pulling off his boots and heavy jacket, he slung the rope around his waist, tying a knot, then securing the other end to a tree, praying, just praying there would be enough length. And if there wasn't?

The rope would come off.

A tiny voice of reason was attempting to make itself heard, a tiny nagging voice that told him not to take stupid risks, that it was pointless losing two lives instead of one. But instinct was taking over now, and he felt no fear, only a sense of urgency as the bridge finally snapped, the Jeep lurching sideways, tossing in the foam like a child's toy. Noah dove after it.

There could be a family in there, a mom and dad, kids….

Please, God, no.

He forced himself to ignore the sting of water in his nostrils, choking him as he attempted to breathe, struggling to stay above the churning black water. His legs felt like lead. Every breath hurt now, and his pulse pounded in his ears as he fought his way to the vehicle. Relief clutched him when he saw the Jeep bobbing on the surface of the roiling river, but the back of the vehicle was dipping dangerously. Water gushing in through a broken rear window would soon drag the Jeep and its passengers under.

The rope tightened around Noah's waist as he drew close, pulling him back as he inched forward. The voice of reason could go talk to someone who was listening. Noah yanked at the knot, discarding his lifeline with barely a thought. He swam the last couple of yards with renewed energy. Feeling the solid metal of the hood on his cold fingers, Noah took a moment to regroup. He squinted his eyes against the rain and the waves to see who was in the car. Noah almost released his grip as the shock of recognition hit.

Chocolate Girl.

She was unconscious, those delicious velvet eyes closed now, blissfully oblivious to the danger that surrounded her. The water gushing in at an alarming rate was already up to her waist. He had to get her out, and fast! He pounded on the windshield with his shoulders until it finally gave way. His hands cleared away the splintered glass until he could reach in. A furious bundle of black fur bit through his sleeve as he grappled with the seat belt and somehow managed to drag the limp, rag-doll body up onto the hood. He held her tight as he rolled them both sideways, knowing they had to get away from the vehicle before it sank beneath the surface, taking them both down with it.

Keeping her head above the water wasn't an option when seconds mattered. Taking a huge gulp of rain-lashed air, Noah wrapped an arm around her and lunged into the water in a less-than-graceful dive, propelling them forward with his strong legs, calling on energy reserves that long ago should have been depleted. Only when they were marginally safer, away from the vacuum that had tugged possessively at them as the Jeep sank to the murky depths, did he rise to the surface. Pulling her up beside him, he gulped at the delicious air and snagged a piece of driftwood, blessedly allowing it to take some of their weight so he could assess how she was doing.

Fear churned in him as he eyed her darkening lips and blank eyes. His legs furiously cycled below the water's surface just to keep them afloat, even with the driftwood. Placing his mouth over her slack blue lips, he pinched her nostrils shut and exhaled his own life force into her, once, twice, three times. Kicking free of the driftwood, he cupped her chin in his hand and propelled them both toward the riverbank.

The sweet feel of the muddied riverbank beneath his feet went unacknowledged. Instead, he rolled her onto her back, ripping at the navy jacket with numb fingers, watching for the rise and fall of her chest as his fingers deftly palpated her neck. The flickering pulse was still there, and arching her head backward, he pinched her nostrils and breathed into her again. When a violent coughing spasm engulfed her body, he rolled her onto her side and watched as her darkening lips turned pale. The cough turned to gulping breaths until finally she was breathing on her own.

Only then did Noah collapse beside her. He closed his eyes for a moment, coughing the filthy water out of his bursting lungs. But they weren't out of danger yet. The river was dangerously high now, and at any moment would overflow its banks, trapping them.

"Hey!" If he'd had the energy, he would have reached a hand out to pat the black sodden bundle that hauled its way out of the murky waters and up the riverbank, stopping only for one quick shake before running over and nudging a black nose at its precious mistress, willing her to wake up. "She'll be okay." Dragging himself up to his knees, Noah went to comfort the animal, but it was a wasted gesture. The dog snarled at him, its dark eyes blazing and top lip curling. But Noah was way too used to angry, frightened animals to be intimidated.

"Is that all the thanks I get?"

He looked at the woman himself. The nasty laceration on her left cheek was void of blood, a telling sign that her body was in shock. She needed warmth and medical help. This nightmare wasn't over. In just the short time they had been here, the river had risen dramatically, and it was already lapping at his boots. If they didn't move now, they'd be stuck in a tree for the duration.

Get her to Mitch, get her back into town. Over and over the words resounded in his head as he dragged his fatigued body to a standing position. But one look at the river and Noah knew that option was now closed to him. And unless he got the hell out of here now, they wouldn't even make it back to the clinic.

It was all the motivation he needed. Noah scooped her up into his arms and carried her along the muddy riverbank toward his van. After sliding her limp body into the passenger seat, he flew around the other side as her faithful dog jumped in beside her. Once in the driver's seat, Noah rested her head in his lap and started the engine, ignoring the snarls of the dog. Driving at breakneck speed was too dangerous in these treacherous conditions, but hell, Noah would give it a try.

There was now no chance of getting back to town.

In his rearview mirror he could see the roads disappearing behind him. They looked like treacherous glass as the river engulfed them, but Noah's only thought was to get her home, to get her to relative safety.

When they reached their destination, Noah left the

doors to the van open and hauled her into his arms. He ran the final steps to his house as the animals rather more gleefully made their own way out. Kicking the front door open with a stockinged foot as her dog nipped at his other ankle, he carried her through to the lounge, then laid her gently on the couch, rolling her onto her side before dashing off to the clinic to gather blankets, portable oxygen…everything he thought he might need.

Only Georgina refused to cooperate. She curled her lip and whinnied in outrage as Noah tried to force her into a cage she clearly thought was beneath her.

"I haven't got time to argue, Georgina," Noah shouted, but the horse refused to budge, planting her miniature but overweight butt on the tiled floor and showing too many yellow teeth for Noah's liking. He relented. "You can come to the house, if you behave." Noah didn't have time to argue, and a stray horse, even if she was pint-size, could wreak havoc if left unattended in the clinic.

But even though she was stubborn, Georgina, along with Madge and the little black dog, seemed to sense the seriousness of the situation. Standing at a respectable distance in the lounge doorway, they watched with worried expressions as Noah quickly made his way back to his human patient.

She was seriously cold, Noah realized, his fingers brushing her icy flesh as he placed the temperature probe in her ear. Its reading confirming his diagnosis. She needed to get out of those wet clothes and beneath a space blanket to conserve her body heat. He pulled off her heavy boots and wrestled with the sodden woolen socks, which were obviously designed for a man. Noah blinked in confusion at the delicate feet that peeped out, the coral-tinted toenails, the soft underside of her soles. They didn't quite fit the regulation work boots.

"I'm helping her," Noah shouted as the woman's dog started to growl. "I'm not attacking her, I'm helping her."

Yanking at her pants, he tugged them off, rummaging through the pockets for ID, a MedicAlert card. Perhaps she was epileptic or diabetic…. He pulled a glucose monitor from his medical bag, and pricked her finger, willing the sixty seconds it took to get a reading to pass. He should have thought of this before. She could have been driving around dazed and confused if her blood glucose levels were low. That would explain the chocolate….

The "normal" reading that flashed on the screen blew that theory. Still, Noah consoled himself as he drew her limp body forward, resting her head against his chest and pulling at the sodden T-shirt that clung to her like a second skin, he was a veterinarian, not some MD in a city hospital.

It wasn't his fault he didn't have all the answers.

After she was safely wrapped in a space blanket to raise her body temperature and he had checked her vital signs, Noah finally sat back on his heels and caught his breath.

Unconscious but stable, he thought with quiet satisfaction.

Now it was just a waiting game. Waiting for her to

come around. Waiting for help to arrive. Other than keeping her warm, what else could he do?

The gash that had been so pale was filling with blood now, reassuring Noah that her body was warming and her circulation was slowly returning to normal. He pulled out a wad of gauze and taped it to her cheek, then reached into his jeans for his cell phone. After pushing numbers for a moment or two, it occurred to him that his phone was as waterlogged as he was.

Maybe he was in shock, too. For the first time since he had witnessed the Jeep on the bridge, Noah's own condition registered with him: the chattering lips, the cough that had racked his body since he had hauled her into the truck, the cut on his arm where her dog had bitten him. And he could sit here and wait as patiently as you please, but unless he let Mitch know where he was and what had happened, the help Noah had stupidly assumed would descend at any moment simply wasn't going to appear.

No one knew they were here.

Reluctant to leave her, yet knowing he had to, Noah headed for the hall. Casting an anxious glance into the lounge, he picked up the phone, fully expecting a dial tone to fill his ear. He stood tapping the phone for the longest time before realization dawned: the lines were down.

Noah was too darn responsible for his own good sometimes, and though normally it didn't faze him, at that moment his sense of responsibility threatened to overwhelm him. The mother of all storms was about to hit, he had a clinic full of animals and an unconscious stranger in his lounge, and no one knew she was here.

No one.

"So what are you gonna do, Noah?" Noah always spoke to himself, just as he spoke to his animals. Okay, he rarely received an eloquent response, but at least it made him feel as if there were an adult in the room. "Deal with it," came his response, and Madge barked her approval as he dashed out to the clinic and poured a generous amount of antiseptic onto the bite on his arm and quickly bandaged it. Then he peeled off his wet clothes and changed into operating blues. Turning on the radio for the animals, he rounded up flashlights and batteries as the lights ominously flickered, a sure sign they were about to lose power. He wondered then if he should move the woman; bring her over to the small studio apartment he sometimes used at the clinic. He had the backup generator there. But after a moment's contemplation he decided against it. She seemed comfortable where she was, and if need be, he could work by the beam of a flashlight to repair her cheek, or carry her over to the clinic and do it there. The most important thing now was to keep her still and warm.

WHO WAS SHE?

Over and over the question buzzed through his mind.

Whoever she was, she needed his help, needed her cheek to be sutured and her scrapes bathed and dressed. Gathering the necessary equipment, Noah headed back into the house, wishing it wasn't so in need of renovations, wishing the living room door he'd taken off the hinges in a moment of do-it-yourself madness was back in place so he could close it on the nervous animals that watched him.

"She's going to be okay," Noah said firmly to them. "But right now, I want you guys shut safely in the kitchen."

He might as well have been speaking Punjabi. Madge promptly plonked her butt down on the floor, and the growl Chocolate Girl's dog gave him told Noah that unless he wanted to dress yet another wound on his arm, he'd better leave well enough alone.

"Kitchen," Noah roared with even less effect. He could have sworn Georgina shook her head.

"Okay, you can stay, but if one of you even thinks of coming near me while I'm stitching her, I swear…" His voice trailed off. The momentary anger that had welled in him abated as he saw the concern in the eyes of the animals, all watching, all staring at the sleeping beauty that lay on his couch.

Who was she?

As he gently soaked her cheek, aligned the edges of the gash, sutured it with the finest thread he had in the clinic, the question taunted him.

His first assessment of her back at the gas station had been right. She really was beautiful. High, impossibly sculptured cheekbones were shadowed by long dark eyelashes. Gorgeous bee-stung lips were returning to their natural dark crimson as the space blanket he had wrapped her in slowly raised her temperature to normal. On he worked, taking his time to suture her, achingly aware that this was a human face he was working on. She would have to live with the legacy of his repair.

The lights finally gave one final flicker and died. A grinding stillness fell as everything stopped around them—the clock, the DVD, the fridge. Only the howling storm outside screamed loudly as it drew closer, yet still he didn't move her. Instead, after taking a few moments to stretch his aching arms, he tossed some logs into the fire and positioned flashlights for adequate light. He washed his hands again and pulled on some new gloves, then resumed his delicate task, only pausing every now and again to try to rouse her with his voice, to check her breathing and her pulse, which was slowly strengthening.

Little details that hadn't even merited a thought on the drama of the rescue were making themselves known at the fringes of his attention. Who was this woman? Surely someone was missing her by now, wondering where she'd gotten to.

No wedding ring.

Relief flooded him. Why should it matter? He wondered, yet somehow it did. Simple diamond studs decorated her ears. In fact, everything about her screamed simple elegance, right down to her well-manicured fingernails. Yet nothing about her added up. Nothing in the clothes she wore or the Jeep she drove jibed with this sophisticated woman who lay before him.

Snipping the last stitch, he placed the scissors to one side and took a moment to admire his own handiwork, The deep catgut stitches he had used to close the wound inside would dissolve unnoticed, and if the tiny nylon sutures he had used to stitch her skin were removed within the next four or five days, the scar would barely be noticeable in a few weeks.

She was becoming more restless now, her arms moving out of the blankets. Occasionally she tossed her beautiful head on the pillow as if having a bad dream. Tucking her arm back into the space blanket, he noticed that the face of her watch was broken. Not wanting her to cut herself with the jagged edge, he fiddled with the clasp, then loosened the silver chain and slid the watch over her slender hand. Turning it over, he carefully read the neat inscription:

So proud of you, Cheryl
Much love
Mom

So the mystery lady had a name.

"Cheryl," he gently called her, repeating her name several times and getting only minimal response. But at least her breathing was more even now, and her responses appropriate. Her eyes had flickered when he shone his penlight to test the reaction of her pupils, and she had raised her hand to push his away as he finished cleaning her cheek. He dabbed at the area now with some antiseptic. No doubt the anesthetic he had used was starting to wear off, since her hands again tried to push him away.

"Hey, Cheryl." Pulling the blanket tightly around her shoulders, he smiled down at her. "I'm just cleaning your cheek. You've got a nasty cut there."

Still no response, but Noah knew she wasn't unconscious now, just in a deep, well-earned sleep. And though he'd have preferred to sit with her and reassure her as she came around, there was too much he needed to do, given the approaching storm. "I'm just going to the clinic next door to check on the animals, then I'll be right back."

He turned to Madge. He had finally relented and let the dogs out of the kitchen. "Watch, girl," he ordered Madge as he picked up the dressing pack he had used to suture Cheryl's cheek. The second she started to wake, his faithful dog would come and alert him.

Even with the backup generator, the lights were subdued, and the clinic felt eerie as the animals paced in their cages, unsettled and anxious. It took Noah some time to settle them before he could finally concentrate on Cheryl's dog. He'd forced the little mutt to come with him for fear he'd jump on his mistress once Noah was gone. At last he picked up the loyal creature, but as he did, Noah felt a sinking feeling in his stomach. There were knots of matted hair beneath his fingers, and protruding ribs that had nothing to do with breeding.

"Hey." He gently soothed the trembling dog. "I'm on your side, buddy."

Noah could forgive most things. Ignorance he could understand, and plain stupidity was sometimes enough of an excuse for an unkempt, hungry pet. But the welts that littered the shivering body he held in his hands had been caused be repeated beatings. Noah's stomach turned over. He could hardly believe that the woman who lay on his couch could be responsible for this dog's injuries.

It would be like finding out Santa Claus wasn't real. Okay, he'd been a late learner, Noah acknowledged with a dry smile. His dad had been working up to giving him a lecture on shaving when his mom had finally bitten the bullet and told him that a guy in a red suit with a white beard didn't really climb down the chimney at Christmas.

"No way!" The words whistled through his lips. No way was the woman who lay on his couch responsible for this. Turning on the clippers, he set to work on the dog, bile churning in his stomach as he shaved the matted hair and tended the multitude of wounds, both old and new. And despite the evidence stacked against her, despite the altercation at the gas station, Noah knew that the woman he had briefly met would never treat another living creature with such contempt.

THE FIRST THING her eyes focused on was a rabbit.

A happy rabbit, Cheryl thought sleepily. Nose twitching, tail thumping, it perched on the coffee table, staring down at her. The strangest part for Cheryl was that the vision of the furry creature didn't throw up a single question in her mind, just brought a lazy smile to her lips as she tried to roll over and slip back into the blissful dream she could only hazily recall. And she would have made it if the simple maneuver hadn't caused a loud rustle. Her eyes flicked back open, and she stared in utter confusion at her body, which was wrapped in tinfoil like some Thanksgiving turkey.

"Welcome back to the world." A man with a grim, tired face was looking down at her, a black dog in his hands. The little animal seemed to recognize her and jumped down onto her stomach, circling furiously before nestling in the hollow of her lap with a contented sigh.

"Where am…" Her voice petered out, the cliché to end all clichés right there on the tip of her tongue. But Cheryl wanted to work that question out for herself.

"You're at my home." Clear blue eyes stared down at her. "I brought you here. I'm a veterinarian."

That really didn't help her.

"You had an accident. You cut your cheek and needed some stitches. Just a few," he added as her hand shot to her cheek. "I'll find you a mirror soon, so you can have a look. I would have taken you into the clinic, but it was warmer in here."

"The clinic?"

He nodded. "Like I said, I'm a veterinarian. My clinic is attached to the house. It's called Noah's Ark. I'm—"

She held up her hand and smiled. "Don't tell me, you're Noah." Now she saw that animals were everywhere: the dog lying on her stomach, another one sitting on guard by the fire, birds chirping in a cage, that blessed rabbit still thumping its tail, a tiny horse peering around the door—

Only then did she do a double take. Her mouth opened, but no words came out as she attempted to focus on the most bizarre creature she had ever seen.

"That's Georgina." Noah answered her unspoken question, his eyes following her astounded gaze.

"It's a horse."

"Don't let her hear you say that."

"It's a tiny horse," she amended, shaking her head in bewilderment. A tiny miniature chestnut horse.

"She thinks she's a human," Noah explained with a dry note, "and she's not actually that tiny. She's ten pounds overweight and heading for another coronary. That's why I've got her here."

"At Noah's Ark?"

"That's right." He had a slow, deep, lazy drawl, but every word seemed measured somehow, carefully chosen.

"And it's raining," Cheryl said dreamily, enjoying this fantasy more and more. The man staring down at her was heavenly.

He was six foot four, Cheryl knew that at a glance. From the day she had overtaken her classmates, when height had suddenly *really* mattered, she had been able to estimate a person's height from afar. And Noah stood tall. Despite the baggy operating blues he was wearing, she could tell his body was toned and muscular. Light brown hair flopped over his forehead as he gazed down at her, and she was tempted to put her hands up and brush it back from his face, to stare unhindered into those delicious sapphire-colored pools. For a moment or two, the whys and wherefores didn't matter. It was so much easier just to lie back and gaze upward, to concentrate on the beauty of the man looking down at her rather than attempt to reason why a rabbit's tail was thumping in her ear, why the wind was howling outside and the rain battering the windows. She wanted to just snuggle in the warmth of the fire and stare back at this delicious man.

"There's a flood," Noah attempted to explain. "That's why I couldn't take you back to town."

"So I'm stuck here for forty days?" She started to smile, then immediately sobered as realization finally hit home. A million questions were bobbing on her tongue, but the first one that had sprung to mind still hadn't been answered. "Where *am* I?" Struggling she sat up and pushed away the hand that attempted to press her back down. There was an urgency in her voice now. "I don't understand…."

"There was an accident."

"What sort of accident? How did I end up here?" She blinked rapidly in the semidarkness. "How did we meet?"

"At the gas station." Noah gave an easy shrug. "It was a nonevent. It's no surprise you don't remember. You were buying chocolate, lots of it and a couple of postcards."

"So how come…"

"I don't know," Noah admitted. "But an hour or so later, I was driving back to the clinic when I saw your Jeep on Hansen's Bridge." Those brown eyes stared back at him without a flicker of recognition as he gave the location. "Hansen's Bridge has been closed for years," Noah explained. "There's normally a barrier up, but I figure it had blown away. Still, the locals know it isn't safe. I saw your Jeep…." For a second he closed his eyes, reliving the utter horror and devastation that had swept through him. "I knew you weren't going to make it. Of course I didn't know it was you at the time.

I could just see a dark Jeep trying to get over the bridge and I knew it wasn't going to make it. The bridge collapsed, taking you and the Jeep with it. I swam out to you. You were unconscious when I got there…."

"You saved me?"

"I was there," Noah said easily. "Anyone would have done the same. I would have taken you back to town for treatment, but the river burst. That's why I brought you here." He gave a rueful laugh. "That's why we're stuck here with no electricity and no phone, cut off from the rest of the world. I didn't think to take my cell phone out of my jeans before I jumped in, and if you had one, it would have been lost with the Jeep." He shrugged. "It probably wouldn't have helped. I just heard on the radio that most people can't get a signal."

His explanation didn't seem to have worked. He could see the confusion still flickering in her eyes. Her forehead creased and she slumped back on the cushion, her mouth opening to speak, then closing in defeat.

"You're okay now, and that's the main thing. As soon as the phone lines are back on, you can call someone, let them know what's happened."

She nodded but the expression in her eyes was still scared.

"It won't be long." He was staring down at her, but every word of comfort he uttered seemed only to agitate her further. "Once the phone lines are back on, I can get in touch with Mitch and get you evacuated to a hospital—"

"Mitch?"

"He's the fire chief," Noah explained. "He's heading up the mass evacuation of Corpus Christi to Turning Point. I'm supposed to be helping him. The storm was heading for Corpus Christi, but according to the news bulletins, it's veered off course...."

"Stop!" Her hand shot up to her ears and she squeezed her eyes shut. "What storm, Noah?"

The rain was pounding on the roof, every window rattling. She should have understood what he was telling her, but nothing seemed to add up.

"I don't know anything about a storm, Noah." Tears were filling those velvet eyes now, and she massaged her temples as if willing it all to make sense. "I don't know anything about Turning Point or Corpus Christi or fire chiefs." Hysteria tinged her voice, and the absolute direness of her situation seemed to strike them both.

"Noah," she said at last, "I don't even know my own name."

CHAPTER FIVE

"CHERYL."

Soft, infinitely understanding eyes held hers.

"Your name is Cheryl."

Reaching over to the coffee table, he handed her a watch. Slowly she examined the object, turning it over in her hand, tracing every word of the engraving with her finger.

"This is mine?"

"You were wearing it when I found you, but the face was broken so I took it off. That's when I saw the engraving on the back. I looked through all your other clothes—" he gestured to the untidy pile that littered the floor "—but there was no ID, nothing at all. I assume everything got lost when the Jeep went down."

"That's everything?" Cheryl asked. "You mean that's everything I had with me?"

"Except for this." He gestured to the little dog dozing in Cheryl's lap. "She took a chunk out of my arm when I tried to resuscitate you."

"I stopped breathing!" It was more a statement than a question. Horror flooded her. She'd been in a life-threatening situation she couldn't even remember, let alone comprehend. Each revelation caused a new jolt of alarm to ricochet through her. She fingered the scar on her cheek, which had only now started to make its presence felt.

"Better not touch it," Noah advised. "That was a nasty cut, and there are quite a few stitches in it."

"What's the tinfoil for?" she asked, attempting a smile. "Were you planning to roast me later?"

"It's a space blanket—your temperature was low," Noah explained, returning the smile. "I'll go and get those clothes now."

"MAYBE MY FATHER'S DEAD." The voice that greeted Noah when he returned sounded frail, an utter contrast to that of the supremely confident woman he had first met. She sat hunched over, staring down at the watch she held in her shaking hand. "I mean, why would only my mom's name be there? Why would only my mom be proud of me?"

"Hey, maybe you bought it from a secondhand shop," Noah suggested, trying to take the edge off her fear. "Perhaps your real name's Tiffany and you've got a husband and three kids waiting for you back home." A surge of sympathy washed over him as he eyed her troubled expression. "You really can't remember anything at all?"

"Nothing," Cheryl whispered. "Not a single thing."

"Well, one thing we do know is that you're not from Turning Point." Noah gave a wry smile. "I'm sure I'd remember your face. Maybe you're from Corpus

Christi. That's where the storm was due to hit. They're evacuating residents here—"

"Corpus Christi?" She shook her head in bewilderment.

"Or maybe you're here on business," Noah suggested. "I had you pegged as a reporter when we met at the gas station."

"Dressed in that? I don't think so!" Cheryl exclaimed, gesturing to the pile of clothes on the floor. The flash of humor brought a welcome smile to both their lips.

"Maybe not," Noah conceded. "Hey, you could be a doctor or a nurse. Mitch had a team sent in from California to help deal with the evacuees, and at the gas station you said you were here to look out for humans."

"I said that! Why?"

Noah almost blushed, and was thankful Cheryl was too engrossed in her own problems to notice. "We had…words."

"About?"

"I jumped the line, you were pissed off…."

"Oh, and that sounds like a nurse…."

Noah suppressed the smile that twitched at the edge of his lips. This difficult, wary woman was snarling and snapping like the dog she'd arrived with, but Noah knew that both of them were just plain scared.

"Still, that doesn't explain the New York accent." Noah kept his voice light, afraid that if she knew he was trying to assess her, she'd get her guard up. "Which part of the state are you from?"

"New Rochelle." It was an immediate response, and

he watched as she hugged her knees and clung to that tiny piece of knowledge.

"You're a long way from home, then," he said softly.

"On vacation perhaps?" Cheryl suggested hopefully. "Visiting relatives for a couple weeks?"

"I don't know, Cheryl," Noah admitted. "But one thing is for sure. This is *temporary* amnesia you're suffering from."

"Oh, and you know that for sure, do you." Her voice was brittle but tears were brimming in her eyes. "I thought you said you were a vet."

"Animals can get it, too, after a head injury," Noah said, deliberately not taking offense at her argumentative tone. Behind the prickly façade, this woman was terrified. "And you're right. Given that I'm not Dr. Doolittle, I can't get verbal confirmation of my diagnosis, but take it from me, animals do get amnesia."

He watched as she pleated the blanket, digesting the information he had given her. At last her troubled eyes looked up at him.

"So how do you know it's only temporary? How can you be sure I'm not going to be stuck like this forever?"

"Because you make a lousy amnesiac." Noah smiled, his casual tone halting the rising hysteria in her voice. "Because you said without thinking that you came from New Rochelle, because you're still the same argumentative women I met a few hours ago. Now all we've got to do is wait until the rest of the jigsaw pieces fall into place."

"Jigsaw?"

"A picture, cut up—"

"I know what a jigsaw is, thank you! I'm not completely stupid," Cheryl replied indignantly. "It's just…"

"Just what?" Noah asked. But when Cheryl shook her head, lay back on the pillow and stared at him with bewildered eyes, Noah knew she'd had enough. "You're going to be okay," he said softly but firmly, peeling the space blanket away and at the same time covering her with a soft, warm woolen one. He shook his head when Cheryl wrapped it around herself and tried to stand up.

"Lie down," Noah ordered.

"I don't want to lie down," Cheryl argued, but Noah scooped her legs back onto the sofa and eased her firmly down.

"You're not going anywhere in that condition. If you need something, then I'll fetch it. For now, all I want you to do is lie here and rest, and bit by bit, the world is going to start coming back to you."

"Promise?"

Where was the woman with the forked tongue and too much attitude? He'd have no trouble keeping her at bay. But seeing her like this, so scared and vulnerable, made him want to pull her into his arms and hold her through this nightmare.

"I promise," he said.

"Sorry…" A tear spilled down her cheek and he watched her wince as the sting of the salt hit her scar. "Sorry for all the trouble."

"Forget the thank-you's and sorry's for now. We could be stuck her for a while. Why don't I go and get you something warm to drink?"

She nodded. "I'd kill for a bath."

"Can't do anything about that, I'm afraid. The power's out, and anyway, you're not well enough. How do you take it?"

"Take what?"

"Your coffee." He gave a slow smile. "Silly question, huh?"

He could see the tears still filling those proud, dark eyes, and her full lips quivered. His first instinct was to go over, but he held back. Professional detachment was what she needed now, a chance to absorb all she had so recently been through and come to terms with her memory loss.

"I won't be long."

"Noah."

The single world stopped him. He turned and stood in the doorway.

"Can I be the reporter, please? I mean, out of all of them, that's the one I like the most."

He got the reference instantly, and relief flooded him when he saw that despite her fear, her sense of humor was intact. Smiling, he shook his head.

"Sorry, this is my house, so it's my fantasy. I've decided now that you're a veterinary nurse, looking for work. A very competent veterinary nurse who also happens to be a whiz on Excel."

"I can't really see me delivering calves!"

"That's my job." Noah grinned. "But I guess you're right. I can't really see you hitting it off with Mabel."

"Mabel?"

"I've got a highly stressed sow about to farrow."

"I'm amnesiac, remember? In English, please."

"A neurotic pig that's about to go into labor."

"Yuck!"

"I figured you'd say that." Noah gave a mock groan.

"So can I be the reporter, then?"

Noah nodded, and was surprised to feel his throat tighten.

"You can be anything you want to be, Cheryl."

"HEY, LITTLE GUY." A wet nose pushed at Cheryl's hand. Pulling herself to a sitting position, she dragged the dog onto her lap, smiling at the eager eyes that greeted her. But her smile wavered as she felt the emaciated body. She reached down for her flashlight and felt a wave of horror as the angry welts that littered his body came into focus.

"Here's a warm drink." Noah stood in the doorway, two steaming mugs in hand, watching her play with the dog.

"He's covered in welts...."

"He's a she."

"Poor thing. He—I mean, she—must have been hurt in the accident, maybe when the Jeep..." Her voice trailed off as she ran the beam of light over the quivering body once more. "These aren't new injuries."

Noah shook his head but didn't elaborate.

"This is *my* dog?" Raking a hand through her damp hair, Cheryl blew out the breath she was holding. "You think that *I* did this?"

"I didn't say that."

"You don't have to say anything," Cheryl felt herself

begin to panic. "The facts speak for themselves. This is my dog…."

"This is the dog that was in your Jeep, that's the only fact we know."

"Oh God…." A whimper of terror escaped her lips. "I'm lying here, praying things will come back to me, hoping I'll remember who I am, and suddenly I'm wondering if I really want to know. What if I don't like me very much?"

"Cheryl." Noah's voice was firm. "You're jumping to conclusions here. The simple truth is, we don't know what happened, don't know what or who brought you to Turning Point." Holding out a mug, he waited until she hesitantly took it. "But like it or not, we're stuck here for the next few hours at the very least, so let's not make assumptions. Sooner or later you'll start to remember."

She nodded, feeling lonely and dejected, drawing warmth from the mug of coffee in her hands. Noah sat on the sofa beside her, put the dog in his lap, and with one hand he skillfully, gently massaged the pup's ears.

Cheryl took a sip of coffee, and an involuntary smile wobbled on her lips. She placed the mug on the coffee table, carefully avoiding the rabbit. "I think I remember something. I take sugar."

"Maybe I just make really lousy coffee." Noah sighed, reaching for the sugar bowl.

"I don't want to be the kind of person who could do that, Noah." She gestured to the injured dog nestled in his lap. "I don't want to wake up from a dream and fall headfirst into a nightmare."

Noah looked puzzled. "What dream?"

"This." She looked around the room at the pictures clustered on every available surface, the flickering fire casting shadows along the walls, the ticking clock and this man who made her feel so safe. "The horse kind of ruins it, though," Cheryl added, her tone lighter than she felt.

"How?"

"I think I must be obsessive-compulsive or something," Cheryl said with a wry smile, "and as gorgeous as Georgina is, she kind of messes up the dream for me. I keep wondering if she's about to leave us a 'present.' I just know that would drive me crazy. I know I like the towels hung straight, the label facing away, and I hate the way you stirred my coffee and put the spoon back into the sugar bowl, and I know that if my bag was here, I'd be heading for your bathroom and flossing and brushing my teeth about now."

"I told you things would start coming back."

She laughed at his enthusiasm, still reveling in the tiny glimpses she was receiving of her personality. "My name is Cheryl, I have a dark Jeep at the bottom of a river, and somehow I've become responsible for an abused black dog that I'm sure I'm not the owner of. It isn't really a lot to go on."

"It will do for now." Without a second's hesitation, he stood and placed the dog in her lap.

It was like being given a second chance. Tears of gratitude welled in her eyes as she embraced the tiny creature. That Noah would trust her, accept her word that she hadn't done this, meant more to Cheryl than she could say.

"There's a storm brewing," Noah said. "I should really check on the animals, and as for you…" He scooped up the rabbit in one easy motion. "How did you get out?" he scolded.

His eyes crinkled at the edges as he stared at her thoughtfully. "It's not normally this crazy," he said, gesturing to the rabbit and Georgina. "I didn't want to leave them in the van but I didn't have time to put them in their pens."

"Can the dogs stay?" Cheryl asked, not quite ready to be alone yet.

Noah nodded. "Dogs aren't work. They're purely a pleasure. Try to get some rest, Cheryl. I'll go and make sure the animals are all okay."

"Can I help?"

"I'll be fine."

"Then can I go…" She started to get up, but he put out his hand to stop her.

"Rest…sleep," he murmured, tucking the blanket over her shoulders. "I'll just be next door."

Strange how safe those words made her feel, Cheryl thought. Strange that amidst all this confusion she could meekly lie back and let her eyes slowly close.

And even though she thought she'd be glad to see the back of Georgina, Cheryl kind of missed the little horse and her furry rabbit friend, missed that twitching nose and the magic she'd awoken to. Her eyes closed as she drifted toward a sleep she so desperately needed. And if she were honest, she had to admit that she also missed the man who was walking away, the man who'd created this haven. A man called Noah, who'd built an ark. A man who had pulled her from the raging river.

A man who had saved her life.

CHAPTER SIX

"GUESS WHAT?" At the whisper of warm breath on her cheek, Cheryl opened her eyes. A tired, kind face hovered above hers. "You can have that bath you wanted after all. There's still a tank of warm water left. It's not hot, but some of those scrapes of yours could use a good soak."

"Scrapes?"

"Believe me, you're covered."

"How long have I been asleep?"

"Only half an hour. I should have let you rest, but I was doing a few dishes and found that the water's still warm, so I'm running a bath for you. It might be your last chance for a while. Once you're cleaned up, you can rest while I go and see to the animals. The weather's really getting worse now."

He wasn't kidding. Despite the tape Noah had applied to the windows to prevent them from breaking, they were rattling like the windows of an old school bus bumping along a dirt road. The wind screamed relentlessly as it circled the house and skimmed over the roof, and Cheryl felt a knot of fear in her stomach. The panic she had felt on awakening after the accident started to rev even higher now.

"Shouldn't we be doing something?" she asked. "Shouldn't we be making preparations?"

"Like what?"

"I don't know," Cheryl snapped, unable to suppress her growing anxiety. "I must have forgotten to bring my hurricane guide with me."

"Lucky one of is up to date, then," Noah said evenly. "There's still a couple of hours to go before the hurricane is expected to hit, but you're right—an old house isn't the ideal place to hang out. So once you've had your bath we'll move over to the clinic. It's a newer building, built with this sort of weather in mind. We'll be much safer there."

That was enough incentive to get Cheryl moving.

"Ouch." She winced as she sat up. "Are you sure they're only scrapes?"

"Maybe a bath isn't such a good idea," Noah said.

Cheryl raised her hand in protest. "No way!" Lowering her feet to the floor, she decided that conversation might divert Noah's attention from her weakened condition. She was determined to make it to that bathroom, and it wasn't hot soapy water that was first on her list of priorities, but a rather more basic necessity.

"What do you have to do for the animals?"

"Make sure their water bowls are filled, put on a few CDs."

A rabbit on the coffee table. A horse in the living room. The thought of Noah's menagerie gathered around a CD player, listening to their favorite tunes, seemed perfectly normal at this point.

"Is that it?" Cheryl asked, refusing Noah's arm and attempting to cross the room on legs that felt like cotton balls.

"That and put some heat lamps over Mabel's pen for the piglets."

"She's had them?" Cheryl asked in a strangely high voice, beads of sweat breaking out on her forehead. The room was spinning like a merry-go-round and she clutched at the banister for support, willing the dizziness to pass.

"No."

"So she's in labor, then—I mean farrowing." Cheryl hoped she sounded vaguely in control. Noah was climbing the stars behind her, like some overanxious parent watching a toddler. She was aware of his hand hovering at the small of her back, and Cheryl knew as sure as eggs were eggs that one stumble, one moan and he'd hoist her over his shoulder and carry her back to the couch.

"Not yet, but she soon will be. Hey, are you okay?"

She was anything but. "I'm fine," Cheryl lied through gritted teeth. The top step was in sight now, but it might as well have been miles away. Her legs started to tremble violently and she willed them to move forward.

"Hey, take it easy…." In one easy motion, Noah hoisted her over his shoulder like some New York firefighter and Cheryl almost sobbed with frustration as he started to head back down the stairs.

"I need—"

"To lie down," Noah finished for her. "You can forget the bath."

"Noah, please," Cheryl demanded, her senses returning, thanks to being upended. "I don't care about the bath—but I do need to go to the toilet."

In a second he had turned on his heel and was heading back up the stairs—no mean feat with one hundred twenty pounds over his shoulder in such a confined space.

"Why the hell didn't you just say so?" he asked, depositing her in the bathroom.

When she was finished, she slowly made her way down the stairs, refusing his help.

"Sorry for not cluing in sooner," Noah said, tucking her in. "I figured I'd thought of everything. I guess I'm just not used to dealing with humans." He frowned. "Hell, you could have said something, though. Am I that much of an ogre?"

"No," she admitted. "In fact, you're so damn obliging I was terrified you might bring me some kitty litter so I wouldn't have to take the stairs. Anyway, I'm fine now," she added, "and I'm sorry if I scared you. You'd better go and fill up the water bowls for the animals."

His eyes narrowed slightly. "There's a bit more to it than that."

"Of course there is. I just don't want to hold you up. I know you're busy...."

"Don't patronize me, Cheryl."

"I wasn't."

"I haven't slept in two days, I've been working my

backside off getting things ready, and the last thing I need right now is to be reminded how little—"

"Hey, Noah," she broke in firmly. "I'm sorry if I sounded critical or patronizing."

"I know." He gave her a tight smile but it didn't quite reach his eyes "I'm sorry, it's just…" He stopped himself then and shook his head, his expression grim.

Cheryl knew there was something more going on, and she reached out her hand in concern. "What's wrong?"

"Nothing."

His shrug didn't fool her for a moment.

"At least nothing for you to worry about."

"Now who's being patronizing," Cheryl said, but her voice was gentle and Noah looked up. "Tell me," she urged, then, sensing his reluctance, she joked, "Believe me, Noah, this amnesia is wearing thin. I need to worry about something. Anything," she added.

Noah finally relented. "I've never felt more useless in my life," he admitted. "And the crack about filling up water bowls didn't exactly help. I told you the storm was supposed to hit Corpus Christi—a city north of here."

Cheryl nodded. That much she knew.

"Well, Mitch and I—the fire chief," he added, "we were already worried that the weather bureau had got it wrong and that the storm was in fact heading this way, even before the bureau changed its prediction. I was only supposed to be dropping off the animals and se-curing the clinic before heading back into town to help. They're going to have one helluva night. The poor bastards who came here to escape the storm are stuck in the middle of it now. There's going to be a lot of injuries, people could be killed, and I can't even let Mitch know that I'm not able to get back."

"Mitch will know the roads are flooded," Cheryl soothed. "He'll understand why you can't be there."

"I know that," Noah responded, "but it's just hard listening to the news bulletins, knowing I'm needed, and instead of being able to help, I'm stuck here and there's not a single thing I can do—"

"Except save a life." Her voice cut in, halting his frustrated words. "You saved my life, Noah. You can play it down, pretend it was no big deal, but the simple truth is that if you hadn't been there, I'd have died, and you know that as well as I do."

Blue eyes met hers, and the frown that had marred his features faded.

"Not bad for a day's work, huh?"

"Are you always so positive?"

Cheryl gave a low laugh. "When I find out, I'll be sure and let you know. So when's the storm going to hit? When does it make landfall?"

"Around midnight, according to the news, but the damage has already started."

"What do we need to do?" Cheryl asked, but Noah just shrugged.

"Sit tight. That's about all we can do. There's not a lot I can do for the animals during a storm. It's all about preparation before it hits, especially in a flood zone like Turning Point." He saw the confusion in her eyes. "For example, if there's even a chance of a flood, you have to drive dairy cattle out of the barn."

Cheryl blinked. "Why?"

"Because cattle often refuse to leave when there's rapidly rising water, and you could lose the whole lot. Once they're out, they pretty much stay out, unlike pigs."

"Pigs?"

"They head for home when they're scared. Even if their sty's burning to the ground, they'll try and get back in."

"So your work's pretty much done now?"

"I wish." He shook his head sadly. "The hard part comes after the hurricane hits. Rounding up herds, repairing injuries, dealing with mastitis—"

"Mastitis!"

Her aghast look brought a welcome smile to his tired face.

"Who gets mastitis?"

"The dairy cows. If they don't get milked…" His voice petered out. "You get the picture."

"I'm starting to, and I'm sorry if I came across as…"

"Forget it." Noah waved her apology away. "I was being oversensitive."

"So how about that bath now? I really do feel much better."

Noah sighed. "Why did I have to go and pull such a stubborn woman out of the river?"

"Instead of a meek and mild one?" Cheryl teased. "I promise not to faint on you, Noah. In fact, once I'm clean and in fresh clothes, and if you can rustle up a comb for me, I'll be so meek and mild you won't even know that I'm here."

"I doubt it." Noah grinned. "Okay, but on one condition—I wait outside. The last thing we need is you fainting again."

"Okay," Cheryl grumbled.

"Good girl."

Strange how even the smallest praise from him made her blush; strange that the hand that was tucking the blanket around her didn't feel quite so comforting all of a sudden.

Pleasantly disturbing would be a more accurate description. And from the way his gaze was holding hers now, Noah was feeling the same. His hand tucked away a loose curl that had strayed across her cheek, popping it behind her ear. His fingers dusted her throat as she gave a nervous swallow, and Cheryl didn't need to rely on memory to understand the sudden shift in tempo, didn't need an explanation as to why her nipples were jutting into the blanket as he stared down at her. And even though there was a power-outage, there was enough electricity crackling between them to light the whole of Turning Point, Cheryl thought. Something blessedly simple fell into place in her confused mind. A delicious, primitive instinct reared its head, and in that instant it wasn't her rescuer staring down at her, wasn't the consummate professional who had tended to her wounds, it was a man, and the look he was giving her was loaded with lust.

A bark from Madge broke the spell, and Noah stood up quickly.

"Wait there and I'll see if I can rustle up a new tooth-brush." It was an obvious attempt at casual, but his voice was unusually gruff.

"Sweet talker," Cheryl called to his departing back, making her own effort to keep things light, trying to sound as if the last couple of moments hadn't taken place, because it was easier to joke.

Easier to keep things light. Easier than facing the truth.

A storm was brewing and about to make landfall—but on both sides of the window.

Something had to give.

CHAPTER SEVEN

IT WAS LIKE glimpsing heaven.

Candles were everywhere, flickering around the sink and tub; Cheryl stepped inside, a curious scent she couldn't place teased her nostrils.

"Eucalyptus?"

She watched Noah's strong hands curve through the water, working the lather into foam.

"Close," he said. "It's from Australia, so you're in the right country at least. This is tea-tree oil."

"The stuff they use to treat nits!" Cheryl shuddered. "You're not about to tell me that you found a few when you were examining me?"

"It's an antiseptic, as well." Noah laughed at her horrified expression. "And it also has healing and soothing properties. I use it a lot."

"On the animals?"

"On myself, too." He grinned at the rather startled note in her voice. "It's good for minor cuts, and you've got more than your fair share."

Cheryl clutched the blanket around her breasts, but darkening bruises and cuts were visible on her arms and exposed shoulders.

Noah moved toward her, his hand extended, then drew back. Clearing his throat, he stood stock-still. "That looks sore. I put some lavender in, as well. It will take away the tea-tree smell, but it's also supposed to…"

"Relax you," she finished, feeling oddly nervous. The blanket slipped, revealing more than a glimpse of cleavage, but thankfully Noah's reflexes were like lightning. His warm hand finally made contact as he caught the blanket, saving her dignity. But the effect of his touch on her naked skin thrilled her more than it should have.

Noah was obviously struggling with his own response. Snatching his hand back, he was backing quickly out of the bathroom.

"Enjoy," he croaked, practically out the door now.

For reasons she couldn't explain, Cheryl wanted to prolong his departure, when only a short while ago, she'd have given anything to be left alone.

"It's beautiful, Noah—the bathroom, I mean." The comment was sincere. A huge claw-foot bath stood in the middle of a vast room, and the fixtures and fittings were all antique.

"Everything looks better by candlelight." He cleared his throat and glanced away. "Actually, it's the only finished room in the house, so I am kind of proud of it. The whole place needs a lot of work. I keep swearing I'll get around to fixing things up, but so far this is the only room I've managed to do."

"What's this?" Her eyes were drawn to a dark wooden box that stood on an old-fashioned dresser, and she ran her fingers over the numerous wooden drawers hidden in the elaborate carvings.

"It's supposedly called a Wünderbox," he explained. "Apparently it was my great-great-grandmother's, given to her by her aunt."

"Was she German?"

Noah gave an apologetic shrug but still didn't look at her. "I think her aunt had lived in Germany at some point, but my great-great-grandmother was Polish."

"What was her name?"

"Ewa." Noah smiled. "Ewa Jankarski. But enough about me. You have your bath now and try to relax. I'll just be outside."

RELAX!

Cheryl sat shivering in the tepid water. How was she supposed to relax with branches scraping angrily at the windows, wind whipping around the roof and a six-foot-four mountain of testosterone on the other side of the door?

Who was she and what the hell was she doing here?

The questions had haunted her since she'd first come to, but without Noah beside her, without the quiet assuredness his presence brought, there was nothing between her and the frightening absence of answers. Staring down at her battered body was the scariest part of all. To finally comprehend the very real danger she'd been in and not know what had happened was almost too much to bear.

Pulling her knees up to her chest, Cheryl hugged

them tightly to her and forced herself to take deep breaths, praying for her panic to pass.

NOAH WASN'T DOING great, either.

Pacing the floor like an expectant father in a hospital corridor, he wrestled with the temptation to knock on the door to check if she was okay.

He shouldn't have left her, should never have agreed to let her have a bath.

What had he been thinking?

What if she collapsed or fainted? What then?

He was almost tempted to peep through the keyhole, but the thought of trying to explain his actions held him back until he was sure she'd had more than enough time to wash. He gave a brisk knock on the door.

"How are you doing in there?"

"Fine."

He wasn't convinced.

"You're okay?"

"Noah, I'm fine."

"Not feeling dizzy or anything? You're not going fall asleep on me?"

"I'm pulling the plug out now" came the answer.

"Well, hurry up and we can both get something to eat. I don't know about you, but I'm starving."

She was about to call out a murmur of thanks, but as she was wiping the steam from the mirror, something stirred inside, a horrible memory. Wood snapping. Hands frantically gripping the steering wheel. Struggling to gain control as everything around her fell apart—

"Cheryl?"

She could hear Noah calling her name, a note of anxiety in his voice as he waited for her response. But it was as if his voice were coming from afar now. Her reflection seemed so unfamiliar as she stared back, wiping the mirror again, catching sight of the long damp brown hair that framed her sallow face. Seeing the scar above her left cheek, she lifted her hand and fingered it, peering closer into the mirror and admiring Noah's handiwork.

He'd done a good job, Cheryl noted. The edges were beautifully aligned, and he'd used 6/0 nylon—the finest of threads to assure the minimum of scarring.

6/0 nylon.

The words resounded in her head. How did she know what thread he had used? How *could* she know that? She stared at the scar, struggling to capture images that seemed to slip away as quickly as they appeared. A strangled sob of terror escaped her lips as the mirror steamed up again, as the windows on the Jeep fogged over, as the bridge started collapsing around her. Her hands flew to her eyes and she attempted to shut it all out, to block away memories too painful to visit—

"You're safe."

Strong arms were holding her, just as they had before, and a deep, steady voice was pulling her back from danger.

"Cheryl, you're safe."

"I remembered something. I was looking at my stitches. Somehow I knew the type of thread that you'd used." Sobs racked her body, and she clung to him, her head buried in his chest. She could feel his cheek against hers, his lips gently shushing her as he held her tighter. "It was horrible—the windows were steaming up and the bridge was giving way. I knew I was going to die. I can still feel it, still hear Buster barking." She hesitated. Another memory pinged back and promptly slipped away as horror overtook her once more. "I can remember what it felt like to know for sure I was going to die. Oh, God, Noah, I really thought I was about to die and no one would even know…."

"You're safe." He said it for the third time, only this time she allowed herself to be reassured, to hold on to the one thing she knew in this lonely, scary world, the one thing that was good and kind and safe—Noah.

There was a subtle shift in her response to him. He still comforted her, but as she became aware of her nakedness, the innocence of a moment ago was missing. She could feel his hand on her damp soft skin, was achingly aware of her breasts pressed against him. The rise and fall of his chest stirred her nipples into a heightened awareness, and his breath was warm and soft on her cheek. Like a flower to the sun, she turned her lips toward Noah's, her eyes holding his. There was nothing left to do but close the tiny distance that separated them. Noah seemed to realize that, too, and their lips met with exquisite gentleness, not moving, just touching. Her eyes closed as he drew her in closer, an urgency prevailing now as his cool tongue, as sweet and decadent as candy, explored her softly parted lips. His other hand tangled in her scented hair, and his kiss blazed a scorching trail through her body. Cheryl felt the pounding of her heart, and another distant, insistent pulse flickered to life deep inside her. As the kiss deepened, their tongues mingling, the heavy weight of his arousal pressed against her thigh, and she arched her back. His lips traced the hollow of her throat, moving down to her bruised collarbone, taking away the pain and replacing it with something infinitely more pleasurable. She yearned for him to move lower, to take her swollen breasts, to cool them with the feathery stroke of his tongue....

"Cheryl...."

She anticipated his detachment even before he said her name and she gently pulled away.

"Cheryl, we can't." He was reaching for a towel now, wrapping it around her. "We can't," he said again, as if he were trying to convince himself more than her. "I don't know anything about you, and you don't know anything about yourself, who you are, where you're from...."

"Oh, yes." It was hard to keep the bitterness out of her voice. Disappointment flooded her veins when only seconds before, ecstasy had prevailed. "I could be a drifter, an animal abuser...."

"You could be married, Cheryl." His voice was thick with regret. "You could be a wife and a mother. You could be engaged, getting married this weekend. Who knows who we could be hurting if we see this through?"

She almost wept with frustration. It would have been so very easy to go on loving him back.

But Noah was right.

"We'd be hurting ourselves, too, Cheryl." His eyes were imploring her to understand. "If we take things further, what's going to happen when we have to say goodbye?" His voice was firmer now. "I should never have let things go so far. It was never my intention when I came in. I heard you call out… I thought you were…"

"Don't be sorry." She forced a gentle smile. "It was a kiss, Noah, that's all. And if my name is really Tiffany, if your prediction comes true and I'm married with three kids, then…" She gave a small shrug. "Well, given the circumstances, one tiny kiss is hardly grounds for divorce."

"You understand why I had to stop things?"

Cheryl gave a reluctant nod, but forced a bright smile. "Let's forget it happened."

But it wasn't just a kiss for Cheryl. Trying to go back, to rewind a few moments and erase what had just taken place was like asking for the moon to be taken down and packed away. She could still taste him, feel the warmth on her back where his hand had caressed her skin. He walked out of the bathroom and she quickly dragged a comb through her hair and dressed in the surgical blues he'd left for her. Blowing out the candles and walking out of the bathroom herself as if nothing had taken place was the hardest feat imaginable.

Cheryl held on to the banister as his flashlight guided her down the stairs. The storm was stirring up more than just emotions now. The sky was black outside, the wind screeched a haunting melody and not for the first time that day, Cheryl felt real fear.

"It's getting close." Noah's face was grim in the beam of the flashlight, shadows sharpening his cheekbones. "We'd better move into the clinic now." Picking up the portable radio, he headed for the window and took one last look outside.

Cheryl joined him, staring in nervous awe at the ominous sky. Trees were bending like rubber, and belts of rain were lashing the windows so fiercely, Cheryl found herself stepping back.

As Noah stared out at the black swirling landscape, Cheryl could feel the tension emanating from him.

"The animals will be terrified," he said.

"They're safe, though."

Noah shrugged. "The ones I've got here are." Still he stared out the window. "It's the ones I don't know about that worry me. A storm panics animals much the same way fireworks do. Unless they've been trained to cope, storms just send them into a frenzy of panic. They lose all sense of reality. Tiny dogs jump huge fences, and if they can't do that, then they'll burrow their way out. Cats are the same. Their instinct tells them to run and they just keep going, trying to outrun the storm. By the time they stop, they're bruised and fractured, exhausted and thirsty." He looked over at her and smiled. "A bit like I found you."

"You really care about them, don't you." She realized her words might have sounded patronizing again, but Noah just smiled, finally closing the curtain.

"They're easy to love. No matter what you've done, what sort of day you've had, they treat you the same.

As long as you love them, they just keep right on loving you back. Come on. I'll lock up the dogs and then I'll get you set up—"

"Aren't they staying with us?"

Noah shook his head. "They'll be safer locked up."

"Can I help?"

"You just rest." Leading the way to the clinic, he called over his shoulder, "You'll be okay on your own, won't you?"

It was more a statement than a question, and given her attitude before, Cheryl could forgive him the assumption. Under any other circumstance, she'd have nodded to his back, would have lied through her teeth and given an easy "sure." But she didn't want to be on her own now. The intensity of the storm was increasing with every passing moment, and Cheryl took a deep breath, not quite sure she was ready to admit that right now she didn't feel so brave.

"I'd rather come with you."

He turned and simply nodded, holding out his hand and leading the way in the darkness, through the narrow passage from the house to the attached clinic.

Even though the backup generator didn't allow for bright lights, after the inky darkness of the house, seeing the subdued glow of the clinic was like stepping into the sun after being in a movie theater all afternoon. But as Cheryl's eyes slowly adjusted, she felt herself smile. The wind was still audible, but thanks to the newer, more solid structure of the clinic, it was far quieter here than it had been in the house. "It really is like Noah's ark in here!" she exclaimed.

"I'm not usually quite this full," Noah admitted, whistling to Madge, who obediently climbed into her cage. He had to wrestle a touch harder with Cheryl's faithful friend. "Close, but not quite."

It felt familiar.

She couldn't explain it, but somehow, the neatly organized shelves, the shining silver carts and waiting machines soothed her.

"You're well set up here."

"I need to be," Noah said, his eyes narrowing thoughtfully as he watched her slowly work the room. "I'm the only veterinarian for miles. I have to be able to do everything from claw clipping to major surgery. There's an operating room through there." He gestured to a black swing door. "The studio apartment is in the room behind."

"Why do you need one?"

"In case there's a really sick animal, it's easier to just crash here." He registered her tiny frown. "I'm not talking about guinea pigs with colds, Cheryl. Some of the animals I treat are worth tens of thousands of dollars. For the most part I visit them on the farm or ranch, but every now and then we do some pretty big procedures here. Now," he said, giving her a smile, "I'll show you the Penthouse Suite."

"This place is huge!" Cheryl exclaimed as he pushed open the doors and led her into a massive concrete enclosure that she could liken only to some sort of shed cum stable with massive roller doors. It was empty now, except for an enclosure in the corner surrounded with lamps.

"Heat lamps," Noah explained, heading over. "Piglets can lose heat rapidly."

Cheryl held back and with good reason. The grunts coming from the enclosure were not exactly friendly.

"Oh, good girl!" Noah crooned.

From the unveiled tenderness in his voice, Cheryl knew he wasn't talking to her.

"She's had them?" Cheryl asked. "Without any help?"

"She's a pig." Noah grinned. "And pigs don't know how to use a call button."

"Still…"

"She isn't finished yet." Noah gestured her over. "Come and watch."

Curious despite herself, Cheryl inched forward, staring in something akin to horror at the massive black creature lying panting on the floor.

"Isn't she gorgeous?"

"I can think of a few other words to describe her," Cheryl mumbled. "Are you this close to all your patients?"

"She's not a patient, she's a houseguest," Noah objected. "Aren't you, Mabel."

But as Cheryl edged closer and peered down into the pen, she felt herself melt. Rows of little tails wagged as the piglets suckled, giving out tiny yelps of frustration when they lost a teat then found it again. "They're gorgeous!" Cheryl breathed. "Just exquisite."

"But they grow into that!" Noah said dryly, pointing to Mabel. "And that's what people conveniently forget when they decide they want a cute piglet for a pet. Mabel was dumped on me a few weeks ago, and now

I'm going to be stuck finding a home for all her little piglets."

"You're not going to have them slaughtered, are you?"

"Not with a surname like Arkin." Noah grinned, but he'd lost his audience now.

"Oh, my God, there's another one coming."

"Watch!" Noah said quietly. "They hit the ground running, these little guys. No sooner are they out than they're looking for food. See how the firstborns take the front teats and the later ones the rear. They'll use the same teat to suckle on…."

"Really?" She was enthralled now, totally oblivious for a blissful moment to the impending storm, but Noah soon dragged her back to that reality.

"Come on, we'd better go in."

"We can't just leave her," Cheryl protested. "There might be more to come."

"There *are* more to come," Noah corrected, "but she's doing fine on her own. It's the first one that normally causes the problem."

"What sort of problem?" Cheryl asked.

"They get stuck."

"And what do you do to…" Pulling a pained face, Cheryl shook her head. "I don't think I want you to answer that one. Do you have an assistant, a nurse?" she asked as they headed back into the clinic.

Noah nodded as he set to work, dishing out meds and filling up water bowls as Cheryl wandered around the room "Yeah," he said, "but not for much longer. She just gave me her notice. Her name's Carly. She comes in three mornings a week for planned surgery and I call on her for emergencies. She's great, but unfortunately she doesn't run to night shifts, hence the apartment."

"So she's leaving?"

"Yep! She gets married next month, and she just told me that she's going to be moving to Corpus Christi. It'll be hard without her."

"You'll get someone else," Cheryl responded without really thinking.

"Yeah. I've got to start looking, once we get through this crisis."

"I recognize this, Noah." Cheryl gestured around the room at the lights over the examining table, the monitors, the ventilator, the oxygen tanks and the drug cart. "It all looks familiar."

"You recognized the sutures, too," Noah pointed out, "You *must* have some sort of medical background. Maybe you are a veterinary nurse after all." He smiled. "Maybe you really are the answer to all my prayers."

"So the little lady couldn't possibly be a veterinarian?" she teased, but Noah just smiled.

"Even better."

He pulled back then, and Cheryl felt it. Pulled back not physically but mentally, flipped the conversation back to casual.

"There's no doubt I'll be able to use a skilled pair of hands for a few days once this storm passes."

And even though he was right to keep things casual, Cheryl felt a hollow sadness as she looked away.

"Maybe I've got Munchausen's syndrome," she sighed. "Maybe I'm just a raving hypochondriac drifting from town to town."

"Cheryl, don't." Noah's voice was firm. "The fact you've even heard of Munchausen's syndrome proves you probably do have a medical background. It's not exactly a term on the tip of everyone's tongue. Do you know what it actually means?"

She nodded slowly. "People who make up symptoms, doctor-shop for drugs and treatments, even operations, when there's nothing really wrong with them."

"See." Noah nodded, but Cheryl remained unconvinced.

"How would you know that without some sort of medical background?"

"I guess." Cheryl thought for a moment. "I think you've just lost your vet, then."

"Not necessarily!" A delicious, lazy smile dusted his lips. "Your skills may still come in handy. Have you heard of Munchausen's by proxy?"

"Where people make up stories that their children are sick, to get attention?" Cheryl nodded. "I don't think it's anything to smile about."

"It isn't," Noah agreed. "But can you believe there's such a thing as Munchausen's by proxy for pets!" He looked at her disbelieving expression and laughed. "I'm serious. There's been quite a bit of research done on it recently. People vet-shopping, making up symptoms...."

"No way!" Cheryl grinned back, amazed.

"It's true. Stick around long enough and I'll show you some research on it." His voice petered out then. His toe had inched over the line he'd drawn in the sand and he was pulling it back. When he finally spoke again, he'd adopted a more formal tone. "It will all come back soon. I'm betting you're a warm, wonderful, loving woman who's probably got a whole family waiting for her, a score of people who love her."

Noah was trying to comfort her, but the thought of another man holding her, loving her, had his stomach churning.

"So what am I doing here, then?" Her eyes darkened in terror, fear creeping into that proud, strong voice. "Why am I in a town where no one knows me?"

It would have been easier to not breathe than to stop himself from pulling her into his arms, to hold her for just one more moment, to bury his face in that long dark hair and just hold her awhile.

"It will be okay, Cheryl. Whatever, whoever you are, it will all be okay."

If only he could believe his own words, he thought. It hurt to let her go, physically hurt to finally, gently push her away.

Noah walked around, making one final check on his animals, talking in low, reassuring tones, unclipping the cages and offering a soothing hand to those who were most distressed. But as Cheryl wandered around her eyes were drawn to two terrified ones. Unlike the other animals, who were making their fear loudly known, this poor creature was shivering in a large cage on the floor, her whole body trembling with terror.

"Georgina." In an instant, Cheryl was down on the floor, fiddling with the latch.

"Watch out," Noah warned. "She's so scared she's likely to take a bite out of you."

"You wouldn't do that, would you, Georgina," Cheryl said comfortingly, ignoring his advice. Once the door opened, she slipped her hand in and gently stroked the frightened animal. "You're a real lady, Noah told me, and ladies don't bite."

Noah watched as she soothed the animal, one hand instinctively working the head, while the other gently stroked the length of Georgina's quivering body. He had known he was right to believe in her. Cheryl couldn't hurt a fly, let alone an innocent animal.

"Let's go and get something to eat," he said.

Cheryl sat back on her heels as Noah pushed Georgina back from the door and closed the cage.

"She's terrified, Noah."

"They all are," Noah said, "and we're probably making things worse by disturbing them. That's why we should head into the apartment. They sense our nervousness, too. They're safe, they're warm and they've got food, music and one another."

Cheryl nodded and let him help her to her feet, but her eyes lingered on the shivering Georgina. "Shouldn't she be with us?" she asked, "I mean, given that she thinks she's a human and everything."

He hadn't wanted her to say that. Life would be so

much less complicated if she had just stood up and flicked that delicious hair, walked toward the door without glancing back.

Why did she have to be the one?

And she *was* the one; Noah just knew it.

He hadn't believed it till now. Hadn't believed there was one person out in that big wide world who quite simply could walk into your life and turn it around, who could make you feel whole with one lazy smile, one gentle touch, but he believed it now.

But he couldn't let her in, couldn't let her sneak into his heart only to have her leave. He'd had a glimpse of paradise. He'd held her in his arms, kissed her, adored her for a moment, but if he lingered any longer, Noah knew his heart would be lost to her forever.

"What about your obsessive-compulsive disorder?" Noah said, attempting a grin, trying to keep his voice nonchalant.

"I guess I could make a concession." Those velvet eyes met his. "We can't leave her here, Noah. She'll have a coronary. You said she was heading for another one."

"There's a hurricane due to make landfall," Noah said firmly, taking charge, slamming mental doors shut just as fast as he could. "Now's not the time to bend the rules."

And they both knew he wasn't talking about just the animals.

CHAPTER EIGHT

"YUM." Cheryl didn't hesitate when Noah unscrewed the thermos and offered her some more soup. "That's the best chicken soup I've ever tasted."

"Can't beat homemade," Noah agreed. "This was down payment for a lumpectomy on a goat."

"Double yum." Cheryl grimaced. "Do a lot of your clients pay you in food?"

"Thankfully." Noah nodded. "There aren't many fast-food outlets in Turning Point. If it weren't for the end-less casseroles, eggs and soups, I'd be living on instant noodles."

They were making small talk and Cheryl knew it. Both were trying to ignore the fact that practically the only thing in the room, apart from a computer, a kettle, a miniature horse that had finally been admitted and a toaster, was the vast double bed they were sitting on, and they had the longest night of their lives to get through. A thick skylight, one of several in the clinic, was above the bed, and though Noah had assured her it was built to withstand even the fiercest of storms, Cheryl wasn't entirely convinced, and glanced up anxiously every now and then. The portable radio had long since given up playing soothing music between news bulletins and weather reports. Instead, the airwaves were filled with urgent reports of flooding, buildings collapsing, trees blocking roads…lives on the line.

"We're safe here, Cheryl," Noah said for what must have been the hundredth time. "It was built to withstand—"

"I know," Cheryl interrupted. "And I know we're probably in the safest place in Turning Point, but tell me, just how many hurricanes have you sat out in here, Noah?"

There wasn't a shred of reassurance in his lack of response.

"Why couldn't you just have lied and said loads?" Cheryl moaned. "Why the hell did you and Mitch have to go and be proven right?" Her startled eyes met his. "Mitch! Mitch was worried that the storm was heading this way, that the predictions were wrong."

"I told you that," Noah reminded her gently.

She ran a tongue over lips that were suddenly dry, trying to catch the thought that had been in her mind, but it was like trying to recall a dream. It stayed tantalizingly out of reach.

"But *I* can remember it. I can remember Mitch saying…"

"Cheryl," Noah broke in gently, "you're confusing things. When you first came to, I told you that Mitch and I were feeling uneasy about the storm."

"This is *my* memory, Noah." She was almost shouting, imploring him to be quiet as she struggled for recall. "He was worried…" She stared up at Noah, detecting sympathy in his expression. "He was worried about his daughter."

"Jolene." Noah's hands were on her arms now, willing her to go on. "His daughter's name is Jolene."

"I don't know—I don't know her name. I just know that Mitch was worried because he'd sent her out there."

"We should call…" Noah didn't finish the sentence, the futility of his words hitting home. The lines were down, and even if the cell phone towers were working, he had lost his when he'd dived in to save her. And he wanted to know, needed to know almost as much as Cheryl who she was, where she was from, the people that were in her life. Only then could he know if there was room for him. "You *have* to be one of the medical staff from California, Cheryl."

His excitement was infectious and Cheryl nodded back, hoping he was right. "Tell me everything, Noah. Tell me everything you know."

"I have."

"Everything, Noah, the color of my Jeep. You said I was buying chocolate…."

"Lots of chocolate." Noah smiled at the memory. "And don't forget the postcards!"

"What was I like? What did you think of me?" His hands were still on her, holding her, the contact of his skin on her bare upper arms a scorching reminder of what had taken place back in the house. The same thought must have registered with Noah, because suddenly he was letting go, easing back a bit before finally facing her.

"You were…" Noah swallowed hard, his Adam's apple bobbing up and down, not sure how to play things here. How could he tell her the truth? That the second he saw her he was enthralled. That in the hours that followed, till he dived in that river and saw that it was her trapped in the van, she had filled his mind, impinged on his every thought. "You stood apart," he said carefully. "There was a lineup and you were in front of me. Bill had one basket in the place, and you'd taken it and filled it with chocolate. He offered for me to go first. He normally does for his regulars if they're just buying gas and the customer in front has a lot—"

"And you weren't."

Noah shook his head. "I jumped the line and you snapped."

"So what did you do?"

"Snapped back," Noah admitted, "and then I paid. Just as you were being served, I took a call from a client, Jack. His horse had broken its leg…." She was frowning now, sheer frustration etched on every feature as she tried to remember. "That's about it, Cheryl."

"What about my Jeep?"

"I didn't really see it at the station. I only saw you running to it…."

"So what color was it?" Cheryl asked impatiently. "Come on, Noah. I'm the one who's supposed to have amnesia here. What color was the Jeep? Surely you can remember that much."

"No," he said helplessly. "I was looking at you at the time."

"At me? Why? What was I doing? Was there someone else there? Was I—?"

"Cheryl," Noah broke in, and she registered his embarrassment. "I was just looking." He gave a tiny helpless shrug. "Doing what guys do the world over when a good-looking woman runs past, only I'm the only idiot who ends up having to explain himself."

"Oh." Embarrassed, but pleased, she started to laugh.

"I didn't see it till you were on the bridge," Noah continued gruffly. "It was getting dark by then. It was blue…gray, maybe." He gave a shrug. "I couldn't really see. The rain was too heavy, and the ground was really muddy. I just knew someone was in trouble. The bridge started to buckle. I was shouting for you to go back." He was waiting, watching, hoping for something to spark, for something in those delicious eyes to register, but instead she stared blankly back. "That's it, Cheryl, that's all I can tell you for now. Once the lines are back up, once the roads are cleared, we'll contact Mitch. Either you're one of his volunteers from California, or at the very least he should remember talking to you. Who knows, maybe by then you'll remember for yourself. It doesn't all have to happen tonight."

But it did.

Cheryl knew that.

Suddenly it was imperative that she remember, imperative that she knew about her past. She needed to find out once and for all if there was someone significant in her life, because sitting so close to Noah, tension sizzling in the air like a fizzing firecracker, Cheryl simply couldn't bear not to hold him, couldn't for a second longer deny the sensations he caused in her. But someone bigger than them both had other plans right now. All thoughts of romance flew out of her mind as the room suddenly went quiet, the storm stilling for an ominous moment. Hair rose on the back of her neck as Noah stood up and tossed their mugs into the sink.

"I'm going to turn the generator off," he said.

"Why?" she asked, bemused, wanting to follow but too terrified to move. "You never said anything about that before…."

"Because I didn't know then how close the hurricane was going to come. This is going to be bad, Cheryl." Noah's face was quilted with tension. The opening door let in the frenzied yelps of the animals, the rattle of cages as they spun in panic, and not even the absence of windows muffled the screeching sound of the wind and popping of tiles as the storm ripped them from the roof. "This is looking worse than even Mitch and I imagined." Noah had to raise his voice just to be heard. "We don't know how long we're going to be stuck here. We don't know what we're going to face tomorrow."

And even though they'd had ample warning, even though Noah had told her to expect it, Cheryl still jumped when the warning siren played over the radio and the broadcaster's voice insisted everyone move to safety and remain calm.

She sat shivering on the bed, staring at Georgina's petrified eyes. The horse's tiny, fat body was trembling. The poor horse was missing her mistress, but her owner had figured somehow this would be for the best. "It's okay, Georgina," Cheryl called over to her. "It'll pass soon. It's going to be okay."

If only she could believe her own words. Nothing could have prepared Cheryl for the full impact of being so close to a hurricane. The powerful wind that had been present for hours reached a crescendo now, infiltrating walls, dimming lightbulbs, rattling cups in the sink. Noah plunged the clinic into darkness and she couldn't pretend it was okay anymore. A strangled moan of terror escaped her as the world seemed to erupt around them.

"It's making landfall." Noah was back, frantically turning the dials on his portable radio in the darkness. "I can't get a signal."

He gave up trying and joined her on the bed, where she sat cross-legged. Reaching out to her in the darkness, he took her hand, and Cheryl clung to it, wishing she could say something brave, wishing that his hand was enough.

"It will be okay, Cheryl," he shouted in the darkness, and she nodded back, holding her breath, biting on her lip to stop tears of sheer terror. "The clinic was built to take this."

He almost sounded convincing, had her partially reassured—until his shout was drowned by an earsplitting noise so fierce Cheryl truly believed the walls were caving in. From his actions it seemed Noah was thinking along the same lines. Pushing her down on the bed, he lay over her as if he believed the roof would fall in, and she held on to him for dear life as, for the second time in a few hours, she faced her own mortality head-on.

"It's okay."

It was all she could hear, over and over. His breath was hot as he spoke into her ear, their bodies so close she could feel his heart hammering in his chest, feel the scratch of his jaw against her cheek, and she gave in then, just closed her eyes and held on, praying for it all to be over.

"It's okay," he said again after the longest time.

The difference was that she actually believed him, and the tension in their bodies should have been seeping out a notch as they realized they had made it, that the building was still standing, that the storm was actually abating. But as he held her, as they lay wrapped in each other's arms, the tension merely heightened. His male scent filled her nostrils, and every fiber of her body was on high alert, every pore saturated with the thrum of sexual awareness, which had been growing in intensity since they first met, as overwhelming and as fierce as the storm they had just survived, and possibly just as dangerous.

"Cheryl?" His voice was thick with lust, and the pressure of his arousal confirmed the intensity of his desire, stirring her own response ever further.

His weight was deliciously heavy on top of her, a body fine-tuned by the land. Muscles that could never be manufactured in a gym rippled beneath her fingers, and she would have lied just to save herself if it meant she could have him, would have said anything to prolong this moment.

"There's no one else, there can't be…." Cheryl stared back at him. "Not with how you make me feel."

She felt him tense, and knew that her assurance wasn't enough. But these were not ordinary circumstances. Tonight the world was being turned upside down, and them along with it. Smoldering passion ignited as his lips crushed hers; he was almost savage in his desire. His tongue, cool yet hard, tasted her, and his hands sought the softness of her skin. As if by unspoken command, they easily dispensed of their clothing. Noah groaned as he cupped her breasts in his hands, and his lips blazed a trail down her shoulders. Cheryl's breath caught in her throat as his mouth closed around a swollen nipple, suckling her flesh until she arched into him with a need that was primitive. Urgency overrode tenderness, and when his muscular legs gripped her thighs, she tilted her hips up until his arousal grazed her heated flesh, causing tiny shocks to radiate from this epicenter.

The foreplay had started hours ago, and now at last she could touch him, feel him, hold him. His heated length hardened beneath the rhythmic stroking of her fingers, he was as close as she was. Yet teasingly she prolonged the delicious torture, gaining as much pleasure from giving as receiving. His moan of approval told her she was doing it right, and ever so slowly she guided him between her thighs. She closed her eyes and begged him to enter, but a heady rush of excitement cascaded through her as he surprised her. He slid down her, his hands gliding over her sweat-sheened skin, his lips trailing across her abdomen and lower still. His tongue searched her most intimate place, and her thighs trembled as he took control, teased her, caressed her. Suddenly everything was shifting, moving out of her control.

The strength of her orgasm caught her unaware, and she whimpered his name, begged him to stop, but her hands delivered a different message. She thrust her fingers in his hair as a tremor shuddered through her. Before it had completely subsided, he slid inside her, and though she should have been exhausted, she felt revitalized now. She gripped his loins with her thighs and drew him in deeper, elation building as she shuddered toward another climax. He swelled within her, and she could hear him calling her name, crying out to her in the darkness. She called for him, too, holding on tight to the one thing that was good and true and surely right.

The man who held her in his arms.

The man who had rescued her all over again.

"TURNING POINT." Half asleep, drunk on the heady cocktail of hormones their lovemaking had unleashed, she mumbled the words. As she lay wrapped in his embrace, listening as the storm slowly blew itself into oblivion, Cheryl found it easy to feel secure, easy to believe that the world was following its natural course and there was nothing she or anyone could do other than go with the flow, get on board the amazing ride that life offered and lie back and enjoy.

"Did you remember something?"

A tender hand stroked her bare arm; a lazy kiss on the top of her head followed.

"Just thinking what an apt name for the town I ended up in. Turning Point." She lingered on the words for a moment, and she could sense him smiling. "Because whatever tomorrow brings, I know life's never going to be the same again for me."

There was the longest pause. Her lashes tickled his chest as she blinked into the darkness.

"Nor for me," Noah replied, a beautiful honesty in his simple words. "They say whoever comes to Turning Point and stays long enough to taste the water ends up coming back for good, or something like that." He shrugged, but not dismissively. "That's a very loose translation."

"From where?" Cheryl asked, genuinely interested, but Noah just laughed.

"From my grandmother. Her grandparents were the ones who first came out here. It would be well over a hundred years ago now, in the midnineteen hundreds."

"Ewa?"

"That's right."

"From Poland."

"Ewa was from Poland, but Alexis, my great-great-grandfather, was Russian."

Snuggling closer, Cheryl waited for him to elaborate, and when he didn't, she thumped him playfully.

"Tell me about them!"

"Tomorrow," Noah mumbled. "Right now, all I want to do is go to sleep and dream about you."

"And I want to talk, find out about each other. Anyway, how can you sleep with this storm going on?"

"Easily. I'm thinking of all the work I'll have to do tomorrow when it's passed, and given we don't even know your surname, my guess is it would be a pretty one-sided conversation."

"Tell me, Noah," Cheryl grumbled. "Tell me how they came to be here, why they couldn't leave."

So he told her, holding her close, and she closed her eyes as she listened to his low, husky voice, trapped between reality and a fairy tale, his story slow and measured. He halted at times as he attempted to recall a detail, and apologized every now and then for a gap in a story that had been passed down through the generations of his family.

"My great-great-grandmother was called Ewa. Apparently she didn't want to come to America. She loved her homeland, but her brother had come out several years before and sent enough money for his two sisters' passage, and since she was only eighteen and in those days you didn't disobey your brother, she had no choice."

"What about your great-great-grandfather?" Cheryl asked.

"They hadn't met yet. He was orphaned when he was fifteen. His synagogue had grouped together and raised the money to send him to America, figuring he deserved a new chance in a new life. His name was Alexis—Alex."

"Are you Jewish?" Cheryl asked, not because it mattered, but because she was interested.

"Part Jewish," Noah answered. "Part everything,

come to think of it. Anyway, they arrived in America, and they set out to find their settling point, traveling along Texas's coast—"

"Is that how they met?" Cheryl broke in, smiling into the darkness as she pictured the scene.

"You're too impatient. If you want to hear, you have to let me tell you."

"But they were in the same group of settlers?"

"Yes, but they were also kept apart. Ewa stayed with the Polish folk, the same way the Germans, the English and the Czechs all clung to their own, and Alexis was with the Russians. None of the groups trusted the others, they only dealt with the people who spoke their language, shared their background. The only person who kept the peace among the people was the wagon master. He was something of a legend apparently. He spoke enough of everyone's language to keep the peace, to give directions to forge ahead."

"So how did Ewa and Alexis get close, then? How did they start talking?"

"We'll never know for sure. Even they didn't know for sure! Apparently Alexis insisted that it was Ewa who first came over, offered him some cake, some bread or something, while Ewa remained adamant that one night Alexis walked past their campfire, that he smiled at her and called her over. But whatever story is the true version, I guess at the end of the day…"

"They just knew?" She felt like a child listening to a fairy tale cuddled up, safe and sound, knowing the ending must surely be happy.

"They knew," Noah responded, "but it could never be. Ewa's sister sensed something was going on and forbade her to talk with him, while Alexis was told that a bride had been found for him, and as soon as they reached their destination he was to be married. The elders told them to stay apart, to stop talking, but…"

"They couldn't?"

This time he didn't chide her for her interruption, just nodded into the darkness.

"The wagon train plowed on." Noah's voice lulled her, even though he was talking over the wind. "And like tonight, a fierce storm was about to hit. The wagon master knew what to do. He had seen this type of storm before, so he turned the convoy inland to look for shelter. The storms hit off the coast here. He knew that waves would follow, and if they stayed on the coast they'd be in big trouble. So he picked up speed, leading them to shelter, but his horse lost his footing in the mud, and rolled over, trampling his master…."

"He died?" Suddenly Cheryl didn't like this story so much; it hit her then that Noah was talking about real people, that this wasn't some fairy tale, but a true story. That he was talking about his past, the brave people who had braved unknown territory in the hope of forging a better life for themselves and their families.

"Instantly," Noah said softly, "and everyone in the convoy had respected him, everyone had liked him, and so everyone wanted to do the right thing by him—to bury him in a way that seemed fitting. So for the first time, they pulled together, different cultures merging at his graveside, all the different religious rituals somehow incorporated, everyone respecting each other's grief.

"They never moved on," Noah finished. "Then and there they chose to work together to build a better life, to embrace one another. They realized that even though they were different, deep down they all wanted the same thing. They didn't just turn away from the storm that day, they were forced to turn to each other."

"What about Alexis and Ewa?" Cheryl asked. "Was the relationship allowed to continue?"

"Not quite."

She felt his grimace and could almost see his smile as he gripped her tighter.

"It wasn't that much of a merger, but the elders finally had to admit defeat when baby Noah Arkin was born precisely seven months later."

"Your namesake," Cheryl whispered, and Noah nodded.

"Despite fierce insistence from both sets of families that little Noah was premature, a pinker, chubbier, more bonny babe was never seen."

"So it wasn't quite innocent smiles over the campfire?"

"Apparently not." His voice was growing lazy now, that heady mix of lust and satisfaction taking over. "Try and get some more sleep." He kissed the top of her head and held her just a little bit tighter. "Everything will seem better in…"

Only as his body relaxed beneath her touch did Cheryl realize he had fallen asleep midsentence. As she felt his tension slip away, she began to understand all that he had been through, and marveled at his strength. Already exhausted, he had dived into a river, carried her home and nursed her. Wriggling free, she pulled the blanket tighter over his shoulders and tucked it in around him, staring in the darkness as his features slowly came into focus. The long straight nose. The hollows of his cheeks. That gorgeous face relaxed now in sleep.

Staring over at her bedmate, Cheryl smiled into the darkness, listening to a wind that seemed to sing to her now, picturing in her mind the people who had come before.

CHAPTER NINE

Perfect.

It was the only word that came close to describing the feeling of waking in his arms, the warmth of his body against hers. As shards of dawn came in from the skylight her eyes drifted open, and she smiled at Georgina, then started to laugh as the little horse turned her haughty, disapproving face away.

"What's so funny?" Noah was stretching like a lion beside her, his hand not so lazy now as he gently kneaded her soft buttocks, his arousal stirring along the shivering length of her inner thigh.

"I don't think Georgina approves," she told him.

"Then tell her to look away or it's back to the cage."

"She's really cute." Cheryl stared at the strange little animal. "I can easily see how her mistress spoils her."

"That doesn't come close to describing it," Noah murmured, still half asleep. "I have it on excellent authority that someone looked through the living room window once and saw Georgina around the coffee table with Mary, eating biscuits and jam for afternoon tea."

"No way." Cheryl laughed. "I don't believe it."

"I do." Noah yawned. "Mary knits Georgina hats and

everything. They go everywhere together. Mary never had kids, and I think Georgina started as a substitute baby and ended up as a lifelong friend."

"So how come she wanted you to have Georgina during the storm?" Cheryl asked. "Wouldn't she want Georgina to be with her?"

"They're both really old now, Cheryl. I guess Mary couldn't bear to see anything happen to Georgina, and she doesn't want Georgina alone in the house if anything happens to her. Somehow I don't think Georgina's going anywhere for a while."

"You mean you'll have her even when the storm passes and the roads are open."

"I think so." He was stretching beside her again, his arms up in the air, not bothering to smother his yawn. "I'll take her over to Mary's for a visit now and then, but I reckon I'm lumbered with the little madam for now." He gave a low laugh. "I'll write it off as experience, I guess. Who knows? I can always open a hospice for spoilt, overindulged miniatures horses if business gets bad."

The rain was still pounding, but with less urgency now. Cheryl lay listening to it, cocooned in her own world with Noah. His hands softly rolled her over toward him and she went to him in an instant. The brown stubble on his chin was peppered with blond, and she reached up to kiss him, a deep, languorous, lazy kiss that affirmed the passion they had discovered last night. Reluctantly Noah ended the kiss, dragging his tired body out of the bed and yawning again as he searched the floor for his clothes, running a lazy hand through his hair. If ever there was a moment she wished she could somehow capture forever, it was that one.

Although the rain was steady outside, the terror of yesterday was gone now, and the promise of today stretched before them.

"Don't be long," Cheryl grumbled as Noah pulled on his discarded clothes.

"Hopefully not," he said. "I'm just going to check the damage, find out what the hell that noise was when the storm first hit."

"You're not going outside." The storm may have abated, but the weather was anything but friendly.

"Don't worry, I haven't got a death wish. There will be power lines down and God only knows what else." Sitting back on the bed, he pulled on his boots and then leaned over, one hand catching her naked thigh through the rumpled sheet. "You get some more sleep."

"You need some, too, Noah."

He gave a weary smile. "*I* didn't nearly drown yesterday."

How long she slept, Cheryl wasn't sure but it was a deep sleep. She wasn't even aware he had returned until she felt the mattress shift, heard a long, exhausted sigh as finally he stretched out.

"How are the animals?"

"Good."

"Mabel?" Cheryl asked when Noah didn't elaborate.

"Proud mother to twelve."

"What was the noise, Noah?"

He paused before answering. "Upstairs is completely gone. There's a tree where the bathroom used to be—I guess we might be needing that kitty litter after all.

"That was a joke," he added when Cheryl didn't respond. "There's a washroom here."

"It isn't a joke, though, is it." She could feel his utter weariness. "I'm sorry, Noah, really sorry. All that work you put into…"

"It's just a house." He sighed. "Downstairs seems okay. I'll have a better look when it's lighter. I'll have to put up some tarpaulin till I can get someone in. I guess we've been lucky, really."

He gave a tight shrug, delivered the usual platitudes, but Cheryl felt his hollow sadness. It wasn't just a house; this was his home. The one room he had lovingly renovated had been destroyed, his family heirloom no doubt smashed to pieces. Maybe in the scheme of things it wasn't much of a loss, but that didn't stop it from hurting. She lay quietly for a moment, wishing there was something she could say that might help. Maybe she was a nurse after all, Cheryl decided, because all she could think of, the only practical thing she could offer was to get up and make a drink.

"Not for me," Noah said. "I'd better get back out there. It's getting light enough to see now. I just wanted to stretch out for five minutes."

"Literally! Come on, Noah, you've only had a couple of hours' sleep. Surely the horses can wait a while."

"No, Cheryl, they can't."

There was an edge to his voice she couldn't understand, a warning as his eyes flashed at hers, but she chose to ignore it, genuinely concerned now. He was beyond exhausted; the very last thing he should be doing was going outside.

"Come back to bed," Cheryl insisted, but Noah just shook his head.

"This is how it is for me. This is what being a veterinarian entails. Animals don't care that you've barely slept for three days. They don't give a damn that it's Christmas Day or that you've been out late the night before."

"Are you trying to put me off?" Cheryl asked softly.

"I'm just telling you how it is." He gave a low, mirthless laugh. "Believe me, Cheryl, there's nothing I want to do more than lie down beside you."

"Or just lie down?" Cheryl asked perceptively. "I bet the floor looks pretty good right now?"

Noah nodded, facing her then. "I'm trying to be honest, Cheryl, trying to tell you, right from the start, how it is for me."

"So tell me."

"I just did, and you've got no idea how many women have said they understand and have seemed to…"

"Until your pager goes off at the vital moment?" Moving across the bed to where he sat, she knelt behind him, massaging aching shoulders that were knotted with tension until finally he relaxed a little beneath her touch. "Or until you jump ship in the middle of a dinner party or miss the end of a DVD for the second night in a row? I really do understand, Noah."

And she did, more than she could logically explain.

Somehow she understood that work couldn't always be confined to a single shift.

"Noah." There was bewilderment in her voice and he reacted to it, turning to face her, watching as she struggled to articulate the images flashing in her mind. "I *am* a nurse. I work shifts." Her eyes widened as memories returned, stilted ones. It was like flicking through a stranger's photo album, catching glimpses of someone else's life. Noah's hands gripped hers hard as she carried on.

"I *know* the pressure you're under. I know how it feels to come home late to accusing eyes. I did shifts, came home tired after a long day, and all I wanted to do was rest instead of go out to a movie, but my…" Her mouth snapped closed, choking down the one word neither of them wanted to hear.

But Noah was the brave one. He faced it head-on as Cheryl attempted to slam that mental window closed, the memories she had begged to return not wanted now.

"Your husband?"

She didn't answer at first. Her brimming eyes met his, and when she saw the pain in his face, anger even, as he stared back at her, it was the hardest thing she had ever done to nod at him, confirming their worst fears. His hand dropped hers, his expression aghast at her revelation. "Please, Noah…"

"Please, Noah what?" He shook his head, striding across the room, wrenching the door open before turning to face her. "There's nothing more to say here, Cheryl. You're a married woman. This conversation *has* to be over."

"I don't know for sure that I am married, Noah. It's just a memory, a feeling. I don't knows what's real anymore. All I can remember—"

"Cheryl." His voice was like the crack of the whip, his stance unequivocal. "If you remember nothing else, then remember this. What happened last night was wrong. Until we knew who you were, we should never have taken things further, and I accept full responsibility for my part in it. But I won't be responsible for breaking up your marriage."

"We need to talk, Noah," Cheryl begged.

"It's a bit late for that," he said tightly. "The best thing I can do for you now is put as much space between us as possible."

"That isn't going to change anything," Cheryl insisted. "That isn't going to make this all go away."

"So how do you want me to play this, Cheryl? How do you think I should react? Climb back into bed and pretend that you didn't say what you just did?"

"Of course not."

"Or perhaps you want me to tell you that last night didn't mean a thing, to forget it ever happened? Just what the hell am I supposed to do here, Cheryl?"

"I don't know…." Cheryl never knew quite how it happened, whether Noah froze or she did, whether what she heard first was the footsteps or the frantic knocking on the door, but even before that, panic engulfed her. Sitting up, she pulled the blanket over her breasts and turned to Noah as a frantic pounding hammered the door, then watched in slow motion as he started to run.

She was searching for her own clothes now, pulling

on the same blue uniform she had worn last night. Once she was dressed, she dashed through the clinic. Something clicked inside—instinct, memories, she didn't know what. But this sense of urgency was familiar, and she knew that the pounding on the door meant someone was in serious trouble.

That she was needed.

She raced behind Noah as he wrenched the door open, then gasped in shock as scared green eyes she actually recognized met hers.

"Help my mom," the lisping voice pleaded.

"Flynn!" She recognized him! But there was no time to relish her memory's return. Flynn's screams were filling the hall, the bandage she had so carefully applied sodden on his arm as he pulled on Cheryl to follow Noah, who had already dashed out.

"They're in the car," he said.

She could feel the mud beneath her bare feet and almost slipped in her haste to get to the vehicle. Anguish tightened Noah's features as he wrenched open the back door of the car, no doubt thinking the nightmare of losing Cody was starting all over again.

"Noah!" Her shout was controlled as she pulled open the driver's door. "Noah, it's Beth who's in trouble."

And she was in *serious* trouble.

The engine was still running as Beth lay slumped over the wheel, her cotton pajamas drenched in blood, and it took a second for Cheryl to figure out where it was coming from. She registered the crude tourniquet fashioned from a tea towel around Beth's arm.

"Help me." It was barely a whisper, Beth's pale lips just forming the words.

Cheryl's heart went out to this brave, amazing woman who had somehow managed to drive her babies to safety.

"We're going to help you, Beth."

"The window broke."

Flynn was hysterical, holding his fractured arm, the slab she had applied literally hanging off, and Cheryl ached to reassure him, but there simply wasn't time. Her fingers palpated Beth's neck, feeling the rapid flickering pulse there. She stepped aside as Noah picked Beth up, scooped her in his arms as effortlessly as if she were a child and started running back to the house. Cheryl went to follow him, but whether it was professionally ingrained or just feminine instinct, she first unclipped the baby seat. Walking as fast as she could toward the house without falling, she carried Paul and used the tiny slice of time to comfort Flynn.

"You're safe now, Flynn."

"Mommy was bleeding, there was so much blood. She tried to call Mitch. I tried, too." He held out his phone to Cheryl, and she struggled to keep the look of utter devastation from her face as she saw the flat signal line. "I think I dialed wrong, but I tried—"

"You did so well," Cheryl broke in, "so very well. The phones don't work, Flynn, because of the storm last night, but they will soon."

She led them through the clinic, where Beth lay bleeding on an examination table as Noah set to work.

Cheryl took the two boys to the apartment, where she fashioned a sling around Flynn's arm from a towel, securing it tightly to his chest and wrapping a blanket around him. Then she turned her attention to Paul, who was purple in the face and screaming at the top of his little lungs.

"He wants his soother," Flynn called through chattering teeth. "Mommy clips it to his sleeper."

She did, too. Thank God, Cheryl thought as she unwrapped the baby's blanket, located the soother and prayed it would be enough to comfort him.

"Told you!" Flynn said proudly as the sobs abated. "Sometimes I put it in for Mom if she's having a shower. It always works."

"You're a smart boy, Flynn." Cheryl gave him what she hoped was a reassuring smile and pulled him into her arms to attempt to calm him a touch. "I need to help your mom, Flynn." She felt him stiffen and hugged him tighter. "You have to be very brave. You have to look after your little brother and stay here. Can you do that for me?"

"Is she going to die?" he asked. "Is she going to die like Cody?"

And even though false hope was wrong, even though she couldn't really be sure, this was a seven-year-old boy she was leaving alone, a seven-year-old boy who had already been through way too much in his short life.

"Mommy's very sick," Cheryl said slowly. "But Noah's very skilled—"

"And you're a nurse," Flynn broke in. "You told me you've seen legs hanging off...."

"Lots of times," Cheryl said firmly. "That's why I need to be with her, Flynn. Can you understand that? That's why I need you to be brave and strong and sit here. I want you to hold the phone, and the second there's a signal, I want you to call me in your loudest voice. Can you do that?"

He nodded solemnly, and Cheryl's heart went out to the brave little guy sitting on the vast bed, staring at the cell phone that he hoped would bring help for his mother.

"GO BACK TO FLYNN." Noah didn't even look up as she ran through the clinic and into the operating room.

Beth's body lay limp and pale on the table, her arm held high by Noah as he wrapped a wad of green sterile cotton drapes over the tea towel Beth had used in an attempt to stop the bleeding. Occasional whimpers of pain were the only noise she made as she drifted in and out of consciousness.

"We need to elevate her legs," Cheryl said instead, eyes frantically searching for a cushion, pillows, anything.

"The table lifts," Noah said without looking up. "There's a lever underneath." He slipped a tourniquet over Beth's good arm and slapped at her hands in an attempt to bring up her veins, as Cheryl lifted the bottom of the table. "Get back to Flynn," he said again, more loudly this time. "I'll deal with Beth. He can't be left on his own."

"I've spoken to him," Cheryl responded, her eyes working the room. In seconds she located the IV flasks and giving sets, all neatly labeled. Locating a plasma expander that was suitable for humans, she started to run it through. "He understands that I—"

"He's seven years old." Noah's face was an unhealthy gray, and the eyes that turned to her held more pain than she had ever wanted to witness. "He watched me try to resuscitate his brother and now he knows I'm trying to do the same for his mom. That little guy's been through hell—he *cannot* be left alone."

"I'm a trauma nurse, Noah." Her eyes held his. "I can remember everything now—everything!" she added. Cheryl could feel the unspoken questions sizzling in the air, the pain in his eyes as his gaze held hers, but there simply wasn't time to go there, so instead she shot into assertive-nurse mode, taking action exactly as she was trained to do.

"Everything, Noah," she repeated briskly, managing to avoid looking at him by turning the connection on an oxygen cylinder and trying to fit a too-small mask over Beth's slack mouth. "This is what I do every day of my working life. I've explained to Flynn why I need to be here, that his mom needs help, and if he can understand that, then you can, too."

"But Flynn…"

"Flynn needs his mother," Cheryl said firmly, coming back to his side as he struggled to gain access to Beth's collapsed veins. "And we're going to make sure he gets to keep her. Now, have you got an oxygen mask that will fit better?"

A nod in the direction of some drawers was all the

response she was going to get, and Cheryl located a mask that would provide a tighter fit and give Beth a higher concentration of oxygen. She headed for the IV fluids, checking what Noah had that might be compatible with humans and settling for the safety of a liter flask of normal saline—not the ideal fluid for a hemorrhaging woman, but at least it was something. Pulling on gloves, she pushed the IV pole over, hung the flask and connected it, as Noah somehow managed to gain IV access. The liquid seeped down the line, but they both knew it simply wasn't enough.

"I'll put in a second line before I take a look," Noah said, and Cheryl nodded as she tried to familiarize herself with the room, pulling out packs and making a mental note of anything they might need. Their first priority was to resuscitate Beth with fluids, to stabilize her hemodynamically, before they addressed her injury. "Do we know any more of what happened?" he asked.

"Just that she cut it on a window."

The second line was in, fluid gushing into her veins. Beth moaned in agony as Cheryl attempted to get her blood pressure reading. She shook her head as she pulled off the stethoscope. "I can't hear it." Her fingers worked Beth's wrist, inflating the cuff yet again, straining to feel a pulse as she let the cuff down.

"Her blood pressure's unrecordable, Noah." She handed him the stethoscope to allow him to check, but Noah shook his head, clearly trusting her judgment. "She needs blood."

"I don't have blood." Noah shook his head grimly. "Just saline."

"But she's still losing." Cheryl gestured to the cotton drapes, dark now with blood despite Noah's tight wrapping. Attaching Beth to a cardiac monitor, Cheryl chewed her lip as she eyed the tachycardia on the monitor. "She needs blood."

"Which I don't have," Noah said again, frustration evident in his voice.

"I'm O negative," Cheryl responded. "My blood can be given to all groups." She carried on as Noah shook his head. "It's no big deal. I'm a regular donor—"

"No," Noah broke in. "No way, Cheryl. You're still weak from yesterday, and anyway, I need you here, helping me."

Finally he admitted that he needed her, but even though it was what she wanted to hear, his argument did nothing to sway Cheryl. "One liter of blood won't debilitate me, Noah. You know that as well as I do, and it will improve Beth's chances tenfold."

"No, we'll just have to get her pressure up with the saline."

"So she can die with diluted blood and a decent blood pressure." Cheryl's sarcasm was unmistakable. "For God's sake, Noah, she's got cerebral and myocardial hypoxia with tachycardia. She's prearrest—a transfusion will buy us time."

He didn't answer, just glanced up at the clock. "It's been ten minutes since I reinforced it, and given we don't know when she first applied a tourniquet, it needs to be loosened now. I can have a quick look at the same time. Pull the lights down, Cheryl. There are swabs over there."

She didn't need to be asked twice. Grabbing a stainless steel trolley, she rummaged for sterile packs and swabs as Noah opened a surgical pack and pulled on a gown. He washed his hand as Cheryl set up.

"A quick look," Noah reiterated, dragging a stool over with his feet and lowering his large frame onto it. "I just want to see what we're working with. You be ready with swabs. Check her radial pulse once the tourniquet's off. There are some protective eye shields in the drawer over there."

Grabbing two pairs, she put hers on. Careful not to touch his gown, she slipped the second pair over his face, seeing the lines of tension around his eyes.

"Let's have a look, then."

"I need to change my gloves first."

He waited patiently while she did so, both taking a steadying breath as Noah released the green cotton drapes he had used to reinforce the crude tourniquet poor Beth had made from a tea towel. "Shit." He cursed as he drew back from the injured arm, blood spurting high in the air, confirming what they already knew—the bleed was arterial.

"She's severed her brachial artery." Noah studied the wound as Cheryl skillfully used the gauze. The seconds between her removing the pressure and the wound refilling were the only chance Noah had to get a decent view, and he used it wisely, calling out his findings as

Cheryl looked on. "Has she got a pulse with the tourniquet off?"

"No." Cheryl eyed the pale, lifeless fingers, her body absolutely still as she strained to catch a pulse.

"Okay, I'll try to clip off the severed artery and then we'll work out what we're going to do." He took the artery forceps Cheryl handed to him, and they both winced as Beth let out a guttural moan when Noah managed to clip the severed artery.

"She's coming to a bit—this must be agony." Cheryl moved to the head of the bed as Noah applied a sterile wad of soaked gauze to the exposed wound. "It's okay, Beth. We'll get you something for pain very soon."

Beth's eyes flicked briefly open, her face contorted in agony. Her lips moved as if she wanted to speak, then she dipped back into unconsciousness.

"I'll wrap up the arm if you can get her some morphine. It's over there." Noah pointed to the drug cupboard. "The combination's eight, four, six, two."

Cheryl nodded, but paused halfway there. "Don't wrap it, Noah. The arm should be cooled for better limb viability. That's what we usually do."

He gave a grateful nod. "There's an ice machine in the clinic. If you can grab some and deal with her arm, I'll get the morphine. At least we've stopped the bleeding."

She set to work as Noah delivered the analgesia, wrapping the arm first before she stacked ice bags around it. Not for the first time she marveled at the equipment Noah had available. His clinic was almost as well equipped as some of the trauma rooms she'd worked in.

Except for the lack of blood—

"We've got a six-hour window to repair her arm before she loses use of it." Noah's voice broke into her thoughts. "That's six hours from when she injured it, so let's assume the accident happened an hour ago."

Cheryl nodded at his estimate and checked Beth's blood pressure again.

"So we've got five hours. But even if the phone lines come back on in the next few minutes, from what I've heard on the radio, the rescue teams have already got their work cut out. There isn't going to be a helicopter standing by, just waiting for me to call them. Add on flying time…"

"Flynn brought a cell phone." Hope flared in his eyes, but the grim shake of her head doused it immediately. "There's no signal, but he's got the phone, Noah. The second he gets a signal, he's going to let us know."

"He's seven years old. He shouldn't have to be going through this again."

Again.

Cheryl acknowledged the pain behind the word, but this was no time to dwell on the past.

"Push the fluid through," Noah said. "I'll go and grab the radio, then check the boys and see if I can find out anything."

He didn't await her response, just headed out the door as Cheryl checked her patient. Although Beth desperately needed blood, the elevated legs, IV fluids and oxygen were temporarily having an effect, rallying her slightly. Her pulse was stronger, and her eyelashes flickered as Cheryl gently called her name, urging her back to a world that to Beth must seem so cruel.

"Flynn...Paul?"

"They're okay," Cheryl quickly reassured her. "They're in the lounge. Noah's gone to get the radio so we can see how the roads are doing."

"I didn't know what to do...."

Her head was lolling around on the hard table and Cheryl scanned the room. Pillows were clearly not needed for pets. She settled for a foam wedge and, covering it with a drape, she placed it under the woman's head.

"You did everything right," Cheryl soothed. "You did an amazing job to get here."

"I knew I had to." Beth's eyes closed with the horror of it all, her words coming out in short phrases as her weakened body struggled to draw breath. "A branch came through the window. I was trying to put up some plastic sheeting. I couldn't just leave it."

"It's okay, Beth."

"The rain was coming in, the noise was awful. I just slipped."

"Don't think about it now."

"I can't *not* think about it. There was so much blood, Flynn was screaming—we both were. But you know what that little guy did?" A look of wonder spread over her face, and her voice was a shallow whisper as she tried to speak. "He ran and grabbed a tea towel, told me I should keep the arm up. He'd been along to the fire lectures with Hal. Seven years old and he was telling me what to do!"

"That's quite a guy you're raising." Cheryl smiled. "He takes after his mom." She watched as Beth frowned. "You drove here, Beth." Cheryl's voice wavered with emotion. "I don't know how, but somehow you had the presence of mind to get in the car and drive."

"We nearly didn't make it."

"You did make it, though," Cheryl said more firmly now. "You got your babies and yourself to safety. You did an amazing job."

"If Hal goes home, sees the blood…" She was starting to cry now, and Cheryl hushed her.

"Stop worrying about Hal," Cheryl said firmly. "Right now we need to concentrate on you for a while. I need to ask some important questions. Do you know your blood type?"

Beth nodded, but her eyes were closing now as she drifted back into unconsciousness. Cheryl was having none of it. Pulling Beth's earlobe, she called her name to rouse her.

"What's your blood group, Beth?"

"O positive."

"Are you allergic to anything?"

Again she shook her head, but Cheryl wanted firm answers. "Beth, are you allergic to any medications. Are there any antibiotics you can't take?"

"No." Beth's eyes closed again, and this time Cheryl rubbed Beth's sternum, forcing her back to consciousness.

"Any medical problems, Beth—diabetes, epilepsy, anything we need to know?"

"No," Beth moaned. "I just want to sleep."

"What did she say?" Noah was back now, but waited until Cheryl finished attempting to get a blood pressure reading.

"That she was trying to push a branch back through a window and slipped."

"I wonder if she has any allergies."

Cheryl shook her head.

"You asked?" Noah instantly regretted the question when she flashed him a dark look.

"Of course I asked. She's O positive and she said she's had no serious illnesses in the past."

He took a deep breath, stared at the clock as if wishing it would stop ticking for just a while. "I'm going to have to attempt a repair."

"There's no point." Cheryl's matter-of-fact voice forced his attention. "Not if she doesn't get blood first. You know that as well as I do, Noah. Her blood pressure's sixty over zip, she's tachycardic. She simply won't make it through an operation without blood."

A muscle was pounding in his cheek.

"Like I said, I gave blood a couple of months ago," Cheryl insisted. "Nothing's changed since then. I haven't taken any drugs or had a tattoo, and I haven't slept with anyone since then except…" She swallowed. "Except you, Noah."

"I had an insurance medical last month." Noah gave a tight shrug. "I had all the bloodwork done, and apart from you…"

"Then there's no reason we can't transfuse Beth with my blood," Cheryl said deliberately. Sensing his hesitation, she took a deep breath and played her final card. "I know about Cody, Noah. I spoke to Beth about it, and she told me that everything possible had been done for him. That gave her some comfort. Surely that comforts you, too."

He gave a slow nod as Cheryl continued.

"Everything possible," she said again. "I'm O negative, Noah, and Beth needs blood if she's to stand a chance— we have to do this. Have you got the equipment?"

He took time to answer, first staring back at her before nodding resignedly. "I take blood from animals a couple of weeks prior to planned operations if I think they might need a transfusion." He gestured to a large silver chest of drawers. "You're sure about this, Cheryl?"

"More than sure." She nodded, heading for a chair and sitting down as Noah collected the equipment.

"We should go through to the bedroom, you can lie down…."

"That's not very fair to Flynn," Cheryl pointed out. "Bring me a stool so I can put my feet up, and after it's over, I'll go and have a drink and sit with Flynn while you set up for surgery."

It was a simple procedure, no drumroll or fanfare needed or wanted as Noah slipped the needle into her arm. As the bag filled, Noah tended to Beth and set up for the impending operation.

"It's full," Cheryl called. "You can take one more without causing any problems."

"You nearly drowned yesterday," Noah pointed out,

but he knew arguing with her was useless. The fragile woman of yesterday had disappeared, replaced instead with an assertive, confident woman. But strangest of all, Noah mused as he switched the bag for an empty one, checking she was okay for the umpteenth time, then connecting the vital fluid to Beth… Strangest of all was that, as chameleon-like and complicated as the two Cheryls he had witnessed were, he loved them both.

"DRINK ALL OF IT." Noah's voice was the firm one now as he placed a massive jug of orange juice on the bed table beside her.

Despite her insistence that she'd be fine, the second Cheryl had attempted to stand, tiny white dots had danced before her eyes and Noah had had to carry her through to the bedroom.

"I'm going to make up a bottle for Paul and then we're going to feed him, and while I do that, I want you to watch Cheryl." Noah winked at Flynn. "Make sure she drinks every last drop of that juice and eats these biscuits, and don't take any arguments from her."

"Can I go to the bathroom first?"

"Sure you can, buddy." Mindful of the boy's sore arm, Noah helped him off the bed and led him to the washroom. Once he was safely in, Noah came over to Cheryl, talking in a low tone so that Flynn couldn't hear.

"All I want to do is repair the artery." His mouth was set in a hard line, but his voice was firm now that his decision had been made. "No heroics, no fancy work, just repair the artery to restore blood flow. The vascular surgeons can do the rest. I've done this type of thing before, lots of times, just not on a human."

Cheryl knew he was trying to rationalize things, to talk himself through the barriers he faced. Cheryl knew something else, as well.

She loved him.

"I think we should feed the baby and get him settled before we start," he said. "The last thing we need is to be disturbed, and Flynn will get upset if he's crying. Anyway, you need to have rest and get some fluid inside you."

"Noah…" She tried to meet his eyes, but Noah stared somewhere fixedly over her shoulder. She moved her hand to touch him, then pulled away, knowing words were all she could offer at this point.

"Like you said, you've done similar types of repairs before," Cheryl reminded him. "You've got a well-equipped surgical room, and I might not be Carly, but you're about to find out I'm one helluva nurse."

Something must have reached him—the unwavering support in her voice, the confidence in her own ability— and finally he managed to look at her.

"I could just leave it. I've tied off the artery." That muscle in his cheek was pounding again.

"*I* could have tied off the artery, Noah," Cheryl said. "But unless the phone lines come on now, unless we get her to a hospital quickly, then she'll lose her arm." She paused for effect. "You can do this, Noah. You don't have a choice."

"You do, though." Finally his eyes found hers, but the

earlier tenderness was noticeably absent—no loving look, no warmth in the blue pools. "I understand completely if you want to step aside, Cheryl."

"I'm beside you." She didn't blink, didn't hesitate, just stared right back at him. "Whatever the consequences, we'll face them together."

CHAPTER TEN

"How's he doing?"

There was an expression in Noah's eyes she couldn't read as he stood in the doorway, watching as she attempted to feed a fretful baby.

"Not so good," Cheryl admitted. "He won't take the bottle."

"Let me try."

He took the restless baby from her, and Cheryl watched in admiration as somehow he managed to get the infant to suck on the nipple. She'd been trying for ages, the whole time Noah had been setting up the O.R., Cheryl had been wrestling with a baby who wanted nothing more than his mother.

"How did you do that?" she asked, watching as Paul hungrily gulped the formula Noah had prepared.

"Years of practice." Noah shrugged. "Mind you, this is the first *human* baby I've ever fed."

"Flynn's sound asleep." Cheryl gestured to the little guy curled up on the bed beside her. "He made sure I drank all my juice before he dozed off. How's Beth?"

"Better. The blood did the trick. Her pressure's up and she's more rousable now. I've set up the O.R. and changed into clean blues, so I'm going to give her the local anesthetic. If you're ready, we should probably get started. Do you think we should bring Paul in so we can keep an eye on him?" Noah asked, waiting as he gently laid the infant in a makeshift crib he had fashioned from a drawer and some towels. He offered his hand as she stood.

"He's a healthy baby, Noah," Cheryl pointed out. "If we keep the door open we'll hear him if he wakes. We'll hear Flynn, too."

Still she sensed his hesitation.

"Noah, this isn't ideal, none of this is ideal, but Beth's surgery is intricate. You need all your attention to be on her. Paul's been fed and changed, he's asleep. I can duck out and check on him, but you have to focus on repairing Beth's arm, not look out for a sleeping baby. He's warm and safe and he's got his brother watching over him."

She eyed his worried face in concern and ached to put her arms around him, comfort him, somehow convince him of the confidence she had in him. But Cheryl knew it wasn't her place now, and after one final check on the sleeping brothers, she followed him quietly into the operating room.

He'd been busy.

A massive cart was covered in sterile drapes. On another, packs and suture material lay waiting to be opened once the two of them were gloved and gowned. Local anesthetic and the sedative were already neatly drawn up on the crash cart, and Cheryl checked her patient, noting with quiet satisfaction that even though her pulse was still rapid, her blood pressure was no longer dangerously low. If Cheryl had had any doubts as to the necessity of this procedure, they were eliminated when she looked at Beth's dark blue fingers peeking out from the drapes.

They had no choice.

No choice at all.

As Beth's eyes opened, Cheryl smiled down at her. "How are you doing there, Beth?"

"Scared."

"I know," Cheryl said gently.

"I think I remember Noah saying something about an operation."

Cheryl felt him come behind her, could feel the warmth of his body as he stood over her shoulder, his masculine scent mingling with the antiseptic, his voice tender but firm. She was acutely aware of his hand at the small of her back, moving her gently aside as he spoke to Beth.

"I did say that, Beth," Noah said clearly. "And now you're awake, I want to go over everything with you, if that's okay."

He dragged the stool over again, and Cheryl decided if he ever wanted a career change, becoming a medical doctor should be at the top of his list. Cheryl felt a lump in her throat, watching as he explained the procedure to Beth, calming her, yet somehow managing to impart the gravity of the situation.

"Like I said before, you do need surgery, Beth, and

soon. Ideally you need to be flown to Houston, to a major trauma center, where skilled vascular surgeons can repair the artery and tendons. It's a deep wound."

Beth nodded, no fear in her eyes, all her energy focused on listening as Noah spoke. "But the phone lines are down, and there's only sporadic cell phone coverage. At the moment we can't get a line."

"You know that the roads are blocked?"

"I heard it on the radio. They said it could be a few days. We need to fix your arm, Beth. Not completely, just to get the circulation restored. We can leave the rest for the big guns in Houston." Noah's voice was gentle but firm. "Maybe we'll pick up a signal soon, I don't know. But the longer we leave things, the longer your arm goes without blood flow…"

"I could lose it?"

"You could," Noah said quietly, "and even with surgery there are no guarantees. But if we don't do anything…"

"Then fix it." Beth stared right back at him, her voice matter-of-fact, a stark contrast to that of the vulnerable tearful woman Cheryl had faced yesterday. "Fix it," she said again. "I really need my arm, Noah."

He explained the procedure to her carefully in layman's terms. A local block would numb her arm, and an injection given through the IV wouldn't knock her out but put her into a light sleep. She wouldn't remember anything.

"Can I speak to Flynn first? He'll be so scared."

"Sure," Noah agreed, "but first let's clean you up a bit."

Cheryl set to work, snipping off Beth's drenched pajamas and as Noah had done for her, she slipped some cotton surgical blues over Beth's legs. But given that one arm was injured and the other connected to various pieces of equipment, Cheryl settled for a couple of strategically placed cotton drapes to cover her from the waist up. She hastily cleaned away the multitude of swabs and wiped down the floor. Even though Beth looked awful, with sunken eyes and a drawn face, Cheryl did her level best to ensure that the mother who greeted her son would look a lot better than when he'd last seen her.

"I'm so thirsty." Beth ran a tongue over her dry lips.

"You're still dehydrated," Cheryl explained, "but we can't give you anything to drink just yet. You're getting a lot of fluid through the drip." She looked up as Noah came in, a navy duvet and pillows in hand. Cheryl gave an appreciative nod at his foresight. The homey touches were exactly what Flynn needed now.

"That looks better." Noah gave Beth's good hand a squeeze. "I'll go and bring Flynn in, but not for too long, Beth. We need to get working on that arm."

"Can I see Paul, too?" Her eyes darted around anxiously. "I'm breastfeeding. He's due—"

"Don't worry about that now," Noah broke in, and again Cheryl marveled at his ability to comfort the anxious woman. "We gave him some formula. I've got bottles and teats—new bottles and teats," he added as Beth opened her mouth to protest. "You're in no condition to feed him now. Cheryl's changed him," Noah added. "He's warm and fed, so please don't worry. Just lie there and try to relax. Cheryl will stay with you, and I'll go and get your boys."

"Poor Noah." Beth let out a helpless sob when Noah had left. "That poor guy must rue the day he got us as neighbors."

"He cares about you, Beth," Cheryl assured her, "and when you care about someone, you take the good bits as well as the bad…" Her voice trailed off. He hadn't made a sound, but she knew he was in the doorway. She could feel his presence in the room.

"Hey." Somehow Beth managed a smile. She lifted an arm just enough to gesture to her son, and Cheryl watched as a sleepy Flynn tentatively walked over, Noah's firm hand guiding him. Beth soothed her scared son, then Noah carefully lowered Paul in his arms. Beth rubbed her cheek against her infant's downy head, and all of a sudden Cheryl felt like crying, not just for the beautiful man she had inadvertently hurt, not for herself and the painful memories that had clicked into place, not even for the proud, tortured woman lying on the table. She wept for Cody, a baby she'd never met, a baby who had touched the lives of everyone in the room.

There should be three.

Beth's tear-laced words came in total recall now, and for a second Cheryl shared Beth's pain, her fear as Beth kissed her sons goodbye, then watched Noah lead them from the room.

"READY FOR THE HAPPY JUICE?" Noah smiled when the local anesthetic had finally taken effect, and despite the needle in her forearm, Beth couldn't feel a thing.

"Nearly." Squeezing her eyes closed, Beth took a

deep breath, clinging to Cheryl's hand beneath the drapes. "Tell Hal I'm sorry...."

"Tell him yourself." Noah smiled, then injected the medication through her IV, talking comfortingly until finally her eyes closed in sleep.

The hand that had been gripping Cheryl's slipped free now, and Cheryl tucked it beneath the drape.

"Ready?"

Cheryl nodded. "Ready."

After scrubbing her hands and forearms for the mandatory period, she stepped back from the sink, murmuring thanks as Noah helped her into a gown and tied her mask, then headed off for his own scrub. Cheryl took the time to familiarize herself with the instruments, opening packs, filling stainless steel bowls with saline and attaching a catheter to the suction equipment.

"Can you help me with my gown?"

His request was more polite than that of any surgeon Cheryl had worked with in a long time, but she didn't want politeness from him. She wanted to talk to him, wanted to go over her past, to explain, to pray he'd understand. And she would, Cheryl consoled herself as she lifted out a sterile gown. Once the operation was over, she would talk to him. So instead of saying anything, she did the strange dance that had been taught them long ago, holding the tie to his gown as he twirled into it. But there were none of the old jokes about roses and tangos today, just an aching silence as she tied on his mask, then waited for him to position himself on the stool before applying his magnifying glasses and changing her gloves.

"We're going to struggle with just two of us."

Again she felt as if he were voicing his own concerns rather than reassuring hers.

"A sterile field's essential. I don't want Beth going off to Houston with some raging infection. We'll need lots of glove changes and…"

His eyes met hers then, and even though she couldn't see his beautiful mouth, she knew he was smiling apologetically.

"You've probably done this more than me," he said.

"I've assisted in a lot of emergency procedures," Cheryl admitted, "and I've done my required stint in surgery, but I've never been a vet's scrub nurse, so you'll have to excuse me."

"We'll get there."

Noah took a deep breath, and Cheryl watched as he forced his shoulders down into a more relaxed position.

"Operation commencement 08:05 hours." Cheryl handed him a massive wad of swabs before snapping a cover over the light handle and pulling it down. She positioned the light till Noah was satisfied he had a clear view, then changed her gloves yet again.

Cheryl was amazed at his professionalism as she watched him work, first irrigating the wound and clearing it of debris. Delicately he removed the tiny shards of glass, being careful not to cause further injury. Cheryl dabbed at his brow and moved his glasses an inch up his nose between breaks.

"Now that it's clean, we can have a look at the damage," he said. He probed the artery ends with his forceps, taking in every detail of the trauma, then carefully trans-posed the median nerve as Cheryl tractioned the bicep muscle back.

"I'm going to attempt an end-to-end anastomosis," Noah said finally. "If they want to graft her later, that's fine. All I want to do is control the bleeding and return circulation to the affected limb."

He looked up briefly, and Cheryl could see the question in his eyes. He needed her support.

"Sounds good."

On he worked, again, liberally cleaning the wound to prevent infection. Carefully he heparinized the dam-aged artery. Blood clots were the very last thing Beth needed. Cheryl could only marvel at his skill as he joined the arterial ends, an intricate task by any stan-dard. The sutures he used were no wider than a human hair, and sweat poured off him in the oppressive heat. The backup generator, already overworked by the lights, barely provided enough energy for a breeze from the fan. But not once, not even for a second did he snap at her. Every request was delivered in a polite tone as he concentrated on working a miracle.

FINALLY IT WAS OVER and time to see if the exhaustive procedure had actually worked. Noah nodded at Cheryl to release the cuff to find out.

They both watched in grateful awe as Beth's veins perfused, and her fingers pinkened. Cheryl probed Beth's nail beds, checking for capillary refill.

"I can feel a radial pulse," she cried. "A strong pulse."

"Good." It was the understatement of the millennium, but his work wasn't finished. Releasing the retraction, he carefully repositioned the ulnar nerve before finally looking up.

"I'll put in a drain and do a loose close."

The elation hadn't hit him yet. Cheryl knew the numerous risks that lay ahead for Beth clearly weighed heavily on him, but he worked on, closing the wound for the surgeons who would undoubtedly be following in his footsteps.

"She's waking up." Cheryl moved closer, vial on hand, ready to plunge Beth back into her twilight zone, but Noah stopped her.

"Let her come to. I'm just finishing up."

He applied a back slab to Beth's arm, checking her fingers to ensure circulation was still restored before finally pulling off his glasses and peeling off his mask. He threw his sweat-laden gloves into the bin without comment.

"She'll need vascular obs every fifteen minutes for the next couple of hours."

"Done," Cheryl commented without looking up, counting the swabs they had used. Old school nursing habits kicked in despite the bizarre circumstances.

"I'll cover her with strong antibiotics."

Paul's piercing cries brought them back to concerns outside the O.R. Noah still concentrated on Beth, while Cheryl dealt with the more basic practicalities: changing the bed and preparing it for Beth, then moving Flynn and Paul through to the main house, which looked as if a bomb had hit. Even with the tarpaulin Noah had secured to seal off the stairs, the wind shivered through.

But Flynn, at least, didn't seem to mind. Once he knew his mother was going to be okay, his sparkle returned along with his cheeky nature. The little boy demanded lunch from a frazzled Cheryl as she struggled to convince his five-day-old brother that sucking on a rubber nipple would soothe his hunger pains.

"HOW'S THE OBSESSIVE-compulsive disorder?"

Bottom in the air, mop and bucket in hand wasn't quite the image Cheryl had been hoping to portray, but she managed a wry smile as Noah stepped into the kitchen.

"Cured," she said on a dry note. "What else, after opening the door to a miniature horse who's been locked up in a kitchen for three hours?"

"We saved Beth's arm, though."

The quiet triumph in his voice couldn't go unacknowledged, and she stood up. "*You* saved her arm, Noah, and in the scheme of things, it might not sound huge, but ask Beth in a month or so and she'll tell you just what a big deal it is."

"She's still got a long way to go, though. She faces major surgery once we get her to Houston and she's still…

"Are you married?"

The question was completely out of line with the conversation, and she hesitated, not wanting to give him a yes or no answer when it wasn't that straightforward.

"Are you married, Cheryl?"

She gave a slight nod, and watched him wince as her message hit home. "But I'm separated," she said. "My divorce is due anytime now."

He stared back at her, hope flickering. "Are you over him, Cheryl?"

"No." She watched his shoulders stiffen. "Are you going to let me speak, Noah, before you pass judgment?"

He relented then, gave a small nod.

"When I say I'm not over him, what I really mean is that I'm not quite over the pain he inflicted." When his eyes narrowed, she quickly shook her head. "Not that sort of pain, Noah." Her hand moved to her chest. "He hurt me here, hurt me more than I thought another human being was capable of. So you don't have to worry about Joe crooking his finger and me meekly following. It's been over since the day he…" She couldn't say it here, couldn't stand in a kitchen and pour out her heart. "It's over," she said firmly. "The divorce should be finalized any day now. If it makes you feel any better about what happened, I'll send you a photocopy of the papers when I get back to Courage Bay."

Ignoring her sarcasm, he moved swiftly on. There were too many questions that needed answers and Noah needed to hear them. "So you are part of Mitch's trauma team?"

She nodded. "I moved to California two years ago." Shaking her head, she walked past him, simply not ready to discuss this. "I'm going to check on Beth."

"Don't walk out on me now, Cheryl." His hand was on her arm, pulling her back.

Her voice was bitter. "What? Now I'm nearly divorced, have I suddenly become respectable all of a sudden?"

"Please don't, Cheryl."

More harsh words were on her tongue, but Cheryl held them back, knowing he was hurting as much as she was, that he simply didn't understand why she wasn't falling into his arms, why the fact she was free didn't make things suddenly easier.

"When I heard you were married, I felt as if I'd lost you. It was the one thing I couldn't handle."

He paused, and Cheryl knew he was waiting for her response, but she was silent, leaving Noah to fill the gap.

"Can we move on now, get to know each other all over?" A smile curved his mouth and his eyes pleaded for her to join him, but she couldn't.

"It's not that easy, Noah. You were right to say we shouldn't get involved before we knew more about my past. I should have listened."

Confusion flickered in his eyes and there wasn't a single thing she could say to comfort him. Instead she brushed his hand off her arm and headed for the stairs.

"I'm going to check on Beth, Noah. We'll talk later."

Beth was sound asleep, not from drugs now but from sheer exhaustion. Cheryl moved quietly around the bed, checking each finger in turn for capillary refill, and even though her heart felt as if it were bleeding inside, still she managed a quite moment of pride for herself and Noah, for what they had somehow managed to achieve in the most dire of circumstances. Beth still had a long way to go. More extensive repair would be required when she finally made it to a trauma center, but what Noah had done—what *they* had done, Cheryl acknowledged with a warm glow—had given Beth a chance. A chance to hold her children again in her loving arms.

"Cheryl." Beth's sleepy voice caught her unaware, and perching herself on the bed, Cheryl smiled back at the woman.

"You're fine, Beth," she said. "Your hand's still there. Warm and pink."

"I can't feel my fingers," Beth said with anxiety. "Well, I can, but they feel strange, like pins and needles…."

"That's from the block Noah put in," Cheryl explained. "Can you move them at all?" She gave a quiet nod of encouragement as Beth's fingers moved a fraction. "It's looking great, Beth. Far better than we dared hope at first. Noah did a great job."

"Thank you," Beth whispered.

"Noah will explain later in more detail what he did, but basically he's restored the blood flow. You're going to need more extensive surgery as soon as you get to Houston."

"When will that be?" Beth asked sleepily.

"We're not sure. The roads are still blocked and the phones are out. That's why Noah had to go ahead and operate. In hindsight, it was the right choice. It would be too late by now to attempt a repair."

"I'd have lost my arm?"

Cheryl nodded. "But you didn't, Beth. Just focus on that for now. And that amazing son of yours brought the cell phone with him. As soon as we get a signal or the roads clear, we'll get some help."

"What happened to you?" For the first time, Beth really looked at Cheryl, her eyes widening in concern as she saw the neat sutures on her cheek. "How come you were here?"

"I had an accident," Cheryl said lightly, not wanting to distress Beth any further. "I never made it back to town after I left your house."

"Because of me?" Beth was becoming distressed. "Because of the directions I gave you?"

"Because there was a storm, Beth," Cheryl said firmly. "It was no one's fault, accidents just happen sometimes."

"You're telling me." Tears filled Beth's eyes. "I didn't need this to happen, Cheryl," she sobbed into the pillow. "Not on top of everything else."

"Maybe this is exactly what you needed," Cheryl said. "You're going to be in hospital for a good few days, having the repair and antibiotics, physio. You'll be able to take Paul with you and you're going to be forced to lie in bed and concentrate on yourself for once."

Beth's sobs gradually stilled.

"There will be help there, Beth, counselors and midwives who can talk to you, help you work through your grief about Cody and all the new emotions a new baby can bring." Cheryl gently rubbed Beth's shoulders. "Sometimes things happen for a reason. Maybe that's why I ended up in a river—"

"The river!"

Inwardly cursing herself, Cheryl tried to laugh it off. "I wasn't supposed to tell you that."

"You ended up in the river."

"Yeah." Cheryl rolled her eyes. "Mitch's Jeep and me. I'm not looking forward to facing him."

"He'll just be glad that you're safe."

"I know," Cheryl admitted. "We're *all* safe, and given what we've been through, that's quite something, isn't it?"

"Room for two more?" Noah was in the doorway. Flynn rushed past him in his haste to get to his mom. He slowed down as he neared the bed, though, and cautiously stepped forward.

"Mommy's fine, Flynn." Beth smiled bravely. "Thanks to Noah and Cheryl, and to you for being so brave. I'm sorry I gave you such a scare."

"Can I stay?" Tears were filling those brave green eyes. Now that he knew his mom was fine and the terror was over, he could finally go back to being just a little boy.

"'Course you can, buddy." Pulling back the blanket, Noah tucked him in beside Beth. "We'll be in and out, but if Mom wakes or there's anything you need, we'll just be in the front room."

"Thanks, Noah," Beth sighed, before she drifted back to sleep and Noah, Cheryl and the baby headed back to the main house. And even though there was so much they needed to talk about, everything had to be put on hold. Beth needed to be checked every fifteen minutes, which Cheryl happily did as Noah headed outside.

There were animals to be fed and comforted, damage to be assessed, and despite his exhaustion, a pile of work still to be done.

FINALLY THE DAY was nearly over, and Cheryl decided she could indulge in the luxury of getting clean. This was the closest they'd been to having order all day, Cheryl thought as she headed into the kitchen. Beth's fingers were still pink, Paul had taken his evening bottle without much protest this time and Flynn was tucking into eggs Noah had retrieved from the barn and scrambled on a portable gas burner, before lowering his tired body onto the sofa and finally closing his eyes.

Though the water tank had long since gone cold, Cheryl was past caring. Filling the sink, she splashed herself with freezing water in a kind of frenetic sponge bath. The bruises on her body were purple now....

Hell, she felt bruised emotionally, too.

She'd expected her memory to return in stages, the snippets she'd glimpsed to multiply, but instead, the second Beth had hammered on the door, Cheryl's memory had returned as if it had never left her.

And she didn't particularly like what she saw.

Feeling incredibly shy, Cheryl made her way into the living room, her heart stilling as she saw Noah asleep on the sofa. He must be thoroughly exhausted now. His muddied boots were still on, his head uncomfortably resting on the back of the couch, and though she wanted to talk to him, a deeper instinct told her that he really needed this sleep. She slipped off his boots, guided those tired shoulders down and lifted his legs up, shushing him as he stirred, then pulling a blanket over him. Sitting on a chair herself, she tucked her long legs under her and simply watched him as he slept.

CHAPTER ELEVEN

"WHAT TIME IS IT?"

Cheryl smiled as Noah's eyes snapped open, his wrist flying to his face as he attempted to focus on his watch.

"How long have I been asleep?"

"A few hours," Cheryl answered. "It's nine o'clock."

"Beth!"

"Beth's fine," she said as he struggled to sit up. "I've been checking her hand half hourly. She could probably go down to hourly checks overnight. Flynn's asleep with her. He's going to come and get us if she wakes."

"And the baby?"

"Right here," Cheryl said softly, staring down at the sleeping bundle in her arms. "I should put him down, really. I'm probably getting him into terrible habits, but he's so cute."

"I'll just—"

"Done," she broke in. "I've fed them all, even given out the meds for you." She saw his look of horror. "Yes, I know some of them are on special diets, Noah. For someone who keeps such lousy books, your clinic notes are impeccable."

"You should have been resting, Cheryl," Noah admonished. "You're not well yourself."

"I'm fine," Cheryl said dismissively, saying it again when Noah raised an eyebrow. "Better than fine, actually. Do you realize that nutritionally, you take better care of your animals than you do of yourself? I found the blender down there and all the fresh fruit you give to the animals instead of yourself. I whipped myself up a high-protein smoothie, even added a few vitamins from your stock, so if I start neighing in the night, you'll know why!" She smiled at him. "They're all fine— twelve little piglets nursing away. I wasn't sure, but I put the heat lamps back on...." Noah gave an approving nod. "Even Georgina's in her cage."

"You got her back in by yourself?" His eyes widened in disbelief.

"I did, though I think I added a couple of new bruises to my collection in the process," Cheryl admitted. "For a little horse she's very strong."

There was a long pause and this time it was Cheryl who ended it.

"Let's forget about the animals for a moment, Noah. How are *you* doing?" she asked softly.

"Better. Three hours is the longest stretch of sleep I've had in a while. And you're right—I really needed it. Thanks for letting me sleep."

"Do you want some coffee? I filled a thermos from the clinic kettle." She lowered Paul into the makeshift crib, wanting to put off the conversation they needed to have for just a moment longer. But Noah clearly had other ideas.

"I just want to talk, Cheryl."

He waited as she settled the sleeping baby and made some coffee. She felt nervous when she finally joined him on the floor by the table, knowing that for the first time there were no distractions, no halted memories, nothing to hide behind—just the truth to face.

"How much do you remember?" Noah asked when it was clear Cheryl wasn't about to kick things off.

"Everything. I think it was starting to come back anyway, before Flynn came to the door. I mean, I knew I was a nurse, I could sort of remember Joe—but as soon as Flynn knocked, everything just came back. I can't explain it really. I just knew who I was all of a sudden, the same way you know who you are."

"And who are you?"

"Cheryl Tierney." She fiddled with a long dark curl of hair, circling it around her finger. "A thirty-one-year-old trauma nurse who is originally from—"

"I don't want your résumé, Cheryl," Noah broke in. "I want to know who you are, how you feel about things… How you feel about us."

"Confused," Cheryl admitted after a moment's thought. "Very confused. I figured that once my memory returned I'd have all the answers but instead it's just thrown up a whole load of questions." A soft wet nose was nuzzling at her arm now, and without even looking down, she cupped the face of her friend, Buster. "I found her on my way back to Turning Point from Beth's. I'd gone there to set Flynn's arm. We found out that the storm was shifting and that a couple of rivers had flooded, so Beth told me a shortcut. I couldn't hear her properly. I knew she'd mentioned a bridge and stupidly I assumed that I was supposed to cross it."

"It wasn't stupid," Noah said. "How would you know?"

"It *was* stupid." Cheryl gave a half smile. "I nearly ran over this little guy, or lady, as it turns out. So I bribed her into the Jeep with some of Beth's cookies. At least I know I didn't hurt her."

"We knew that all along," Noah pointed out. "So what were you doing, buying all the chocolate?"

"It was for Mitch and the teams." Cheryl gave a tiny grimace. "How the hell am I supposed to tell him about his Jeep?"

"I'll break it to him for you," Noah offered, but his voice grew more serious as he continued. "I was heading into town to drop off medical supplies. Mitch and I decided that despite the warnings, the storm was heading off course, so we agreed I'd go home and lock up the animals, then head back into town to help out where I could. The hall was all set up. I was going to help out at the triage…" He smiled. "That was you?"

Cheryl nodded.

"Seems like we were destined to meet."

"Perhaps," Cheryl replied, but her voice was wary. She was determined to keep to the facts for now.

"Cheryl, after I saw you in the gas station, you were all I could think about. I didn't know it was your vehicle on the bridge, but when I swam over, when I saw it was you, for a moment it felt like fate."

"Oh, come on, Noah." She gave a shrug. "I had an accident, you were there, but as grateful as I am, I think

you're being a bit melodramatic. If the stars did somehow align to bring us together, I think it was for a rather
more practical purpose." He frowned. "Beth," Cheryl explained. "If we both hadn't been here, she'd have died."

"Hey, what happened to the woman I woke up with?"
Noah asked, bemused, and she knew he didn't understand why she couldn't just fall into his arms the way
she had last night.

"She got her memory back," Cheryl answered.
"Noah, I had the perfect life. I was the eldest. Heather,
my sister, is eight years younger than me. I had great
parents, a great home and later a great job. I met Joe
when I was still in high school. We got married when I
finished my nursing degree."

"Young, then?" Noah asked.

"Twenty-one. Everyone said we were too young, but
I loved him and he loved me, or at least he did."

She swallowed hard, and Noah knew it was difficult
for her to talk about this. He hated putting her through
it, but he needed answers so badly that even breathing
hurt now. Somehow he held back and let her story un-
fold at her own pace.

"It was great for the first three years," she said, "until
I told him I wanted to have kids. I loved nursing, but I
really wanted a family. Joe didn't." Her voice dropped,
and her troubled, hurt eyes met his. "All of a sudden he
said that he wasn't happy in his work. He was an ac-
countanting clerk in a law firm. He said the last thing
we could afford was for me to give up work and start a
family. He wanted to go back to school."

"What did you do?"

"Supported him, of course," Cheryl said instantly. "I didn't want him feeling dissatisfied, so I put the family plan on hold, picked up extra shifts so that he could follow his dream."

"He went back full-time?" There was a slightly incredulous note to Noah's voice. "Why didn't he study in the evening?"

Cheryl shrugged. "He figured he was already a few years behind, and I guess I thought the quicker he got his law degree, the quicker we could start a family. I didn't mind." Not even a trace of bitterness tinged her voice. "I really didn't mind. Joe got his degree. He even got a job back with his old firm—and everything should have been perfect...."

"It wasn't?"

Cheryl shook her head. "I always thought the second he got his degree and started work, that I'd go off the pill, but I didn't." She stared at her empty mug, handing it over as, without a word, he topped it up. "I knew something wasn't right, I just didn't know what. When I said before that I understood about shift work, I really did. Suddenly we were arguing about the fact I worked weekends, arguing if I was home ten minutes late from a shift. Joe hadn't minded when I was supporting him, but suddenly everything I did seemed to be wrong, as if he were looking for an excuse to start a fight."

"Was he having an affair?" He watched her shoulders stiffen, and anger blasted through him, at a man he had never even met.

"Yes, but it wasn't only Joe's infidelity that devastated me."

Noah watched as she tried to hold back her tears, and though every fiber of his being told him to go over to her, he knew she didn't want him to.

"I was heading for work one day when my mom called. She sounded awful, so of course I went straight over. She told me that my father was leaving her. Apparently their marriage had been a sham. Dad had been seeing another woman for years, but they'd stayed together for the kids. Now that Heather had finished her studies, he'd decided there was no need for them to stay together anymore, that it was time to finally be honest." She gave a strangled sob, and Noah pulled her in closer. "I couldn't believe it. It was as if my whole childhood had been a sham, the happy loving family I'd grown up in had all been an act. I didn't phone Joe, I didn't even call into work. I headed straight for home. I just wanted to be by myself. That's when I found them in our bed." Her voice was rising now. "In *our* bed. Noah, I lost everything that day. My family, my husband, my home— I couldn't go back there, couldn't walk in that door after what I'd seen. The only thing I had was my career. Even my name changed that day."

"You dropped his surname."

Cheryl nodded. "The next day. I went to work and had them make up new name tags. I didn't want any part of him, Noah. I didn't want a single thing from him, didn't even want to be in the same town as him."

"So you came to California?"

"It was a great job. I didn't think I'd get it when I applied, even though I had a lot of experience. But they took me on, and suddenly I was on a plane heading for Courage Bay in sunny California. I found a small apartment and slowly got back on my feet. For the first time in years I wasn't supporting someone, just myself, and you know what? It felt good. I refused to let myself go, even though I felt as low as I thought I could get. I joined a gym, took care of myself, ate properly, give or take the odd bar of chocolate." Cheryl gave a small smile. "And sugar in my coffee. But on the whole I found it easier when I was taking care of myself.

"And one of the nicest things of all was that I fell in love with nursing again. I love it, Noah." Her eyes brimmed with tears now, but tears of pride. "It had become a job when I was supporting Joe, I burnt myself out doing extra shifts just to keep our finances in the red, but when I came to Courage Bay and had only myself to worry about, I realized that I was actually really good at it. I'm in charge of a trauma unit. I go to work and I lose myself, focus on other people's problems. And the best part of all is I'm a damn good nurse."

"But it's not all of who you are," Noah prompted softly. "You can be a damn good nurse and still have a life away from work."

He felt her stiffen and regretted pushing things too far. She pulled away, unclipped the watch from her slender wrist and stared at it.

"Do you know why I cried when I saw this?" Her fingers traced each word. "Mom sent me this when I got the job and moved. It was supposed to cheer me up." She gave a wry laugh. "It was the first time I'd seen it written—mom without dad. It just looked wrong, Noah, but I don't expect you to understand."

"But I do." He was quiet for a moment before elaborating. "The first Christmas after my father died, I remember opening my card from my mom. It felt incredibly sad seeing her name written without dad's beside it. It was hard to read and it would have been hard for my mom to write—yours, too."

His insight was almost more than she could bear. She almost wished he would say the wrong thing, offer a dash of callous indifference so she could somehow justify walking away.

"How is she now? Your mother?" Noah asked.

"Getting there, I guess," Cheryl said stiffly. "She says she's happy. She spends a lot of time with Heather, who's got a new baby...."

"And your dad?" He watched her lips thin. "How's he doing?"

"I don't know," Cheryl responded with a note of defiance. "And I don't want to know, either. He's a liar...."

"He's your dad, Cheryl. And from the way you describe your childhood, it sounds as if he was a good one. Who knows the complicated games people play. Who knows why your parents decided to stay together when they clearly weren't in love. I couldn't do it." He paused for a moment and thought about it, but the answer was still the same. "I couldn't do it, Cheryl, but for whatever reason, your parents did. Your dad stayed with your mom when he could have left. Have you ever thought that maybe it was because he loved you?"

"I lost everything that day." Her voice was a raw whisper, his answer too simple for the agony in her soul. "I was a mess, Noah. But somehow I picked myself up, made it through. And I swore then and there that I'd never bend over backward to please a man, never give all of myself to anyone, that the only safe thing to do is keep a piece of me back."

"Keep everyone out, you mean?" Noah suggested, but Cheryl fiercely shook her head.

"My mother wasted thirty years on my father, thirty years of knowing he was cheating…."

"You didn't, though," Noah pointed out. "What happened with your parents is awful, but it doesn't compare with what happened to you. You're stronger than that, Cheryl. You didn't waste twenty seconds on a relationship that was going nowhere. The second you knew it was over, you were out of there.

"Cheryl." His words were soft, but firm. "Surely you know…"

"That you'd never hurt me like that," she concluded. "They're just words, Noah." Seeing the pain in his eyes, she relented slightly. "Look, we're getting ahead of ourselves." She took a deep breath. "I'm just telling you where I'm at at the moment. How since my memories returned, life's a touch more complicated. With what I know now, I realize that we shouldn't have slept together, that things have gone too far. Surely you must see the need to take things more slowly." Noah was shaking his head as she spoke, and he gave a hollow laugh devoid of humor. But Cheryl chose to ignore it. She was determined to get her speech over and done with. "When I get back to Courage Bay, we can phone each other, e-mail, get to know each other slowly…."

"Let it fizzle out gradually, you mean?"

"I didn't say that," Cheryl retorted, but she couldn't bring herself to look at him, couldn't look in his eyes and deliver a barefaced lie.

"You didn't have to say it, Cheryl, but we both know that's what you're thinking—get the hell out of here, put as much space between us as you possibly can so you can get your head together."

"And what are you suggesting I do, Noah?" Cheryl said bitterly. "Call up work and hand in my notice? Arrange a removal truck to transport my stuff here?"

"Of course not…." Noah answered, but Cheryl hadn't finished yet.

"We've known each other less than two days. Even forgetting what I've just told you, it would be reckless in the extreme to throw away—"

"No one's asking you to throw everything away," Noah said. "All I'm asking is that you stay a bit longer."

"How?"

"Cheryl, you nearly drowned yesterday. You're covered in bruises and cuts. If anyone deserves to be off sick, it's you—take some downtime, spend some time here. We can go slowly if that's what you want, but you know as well as I that if you go back now, if you leave Turning Point in the next couple of days, you'll be gone for good. Somehow you'll convince yourself we didn't really know each other enough. You'll lose sight of the dream we found here together. You'll put it all down to your head injury or some sort of bizarre holiday romance, and the farther away from us you go, the harder it will be to remember just how special this is.

"Two weeks," he urged. "Stay for just two more weeks. We'll say you can't fly, that you're nauseated from your head injury. Take a couple of weeks off work and we can have time to get to know each other, spend some real time together, work out what we're going to do...."

It sounded so easy, so logical, and in truth, the easiest thing in the world for Cheryl would be to stay, to hold on to the fantasy for a bit longer. But she needed distance, clarity. She needed to examine her feelings.

"I have to go home, Noah." She was so tempted to waver, to live the dream, bury the pain of the past and look to the future. It was so very tempting and yet so very scary. Somehow it was easier to be angry, to speak harshly rather than allow him to glimpse the indecision in her heart. "And you have to respect that. I'm not going to call in sick just to sort out my love life. I'm more professional than that."

"You're twisting my words."

"Am I?" Her eyes widened. "If it's so easy, *you* do it. If the next two weeks are so vital for us, why don't *you* get on a plane and come home with me?"

"You know I can't. This isn't a job where I can just hang up a closed sign on the door and disappear for a week or two, though believe me, right now there's nothing I want to do more. People rely on me."

"It's the same for me, Noah," Cheryl pointed out. "I don't work in a candy store. I'm a trauma nurse. And as insensitive as it might sound, instead of saying that people rely on you, shouldn't you be saying that it's actually animals that rely on you, Noah? There is a difference. My patients happen to be human. I make a difference every day when I go to work, so don't stand there and try to belittle my career, implying I'm just a nurse who can be easily replaced!"

She knew she'd gone too far even before the hurt flickered in his eyes. Cheryl knew that she had misinterpreted Noah's words, and her response had been unfair. But she couldn't take it back.

"*People* rely on me." Noah's expression was hard. "This is a ranching community, Cheryl. We're talking about people's livelihoods. If I hop on a plane and follow you back to Courage Bay for a couple of weeks without months of planning, then I let a lot of people down."

"And that's the crux of it—" Tears welled in her eyes as she admitted the truth. "This can never work. You know that and so do I. What if I do stay for a couple of weeks, what if this crazy dream does somehow carry on, what then?"

"We'd work something out…." Noah offered, but his voice faded and Cheryl knew he finally got it.

"You're never going to leave, Noah," she said with more than a trace of bitterness. "So better we end it now, cut our losses and get out before we really get hurt."

"What do you want me to say, Cheryl? That I'll walk away from everything I've spent my whole life building?" Anger was brimming to the fore now. "Hey, but then why the hell not? I could work in some poodle parlor, trim a few nails and make a real difference to the world. Come to think of it, I enjoyed treating Beth. Maybe I should head off to California and study to be a doctor, ask you to support me the same way your husband did. Would that make you feel better? Would that prove to you that I loved you enough?"

Angry emotions had been unleashed now, words said in haste that they knew would surely haunt them, but both of them were too proud and too raw to back down.

"You've got this vision in your head of the perfect woman, Noah," Cheryl shouted. "A woman who'll step into your dream world with no questions asked. Accept your bloody clinic because it's your life, and heaven help her if she dares to question it. Heaven help her if she decides it's not where she wants to be."

"You wanted to be here, Cheryl," Noah roared back. "The Cheryl that lay on that couch last night wanted to be here."

"That was yesterday."

"That was you!" His shout petered out midway, replaced with a rasping plea for her to listen. "That was you," he said more softly. "The real Cheryl, the Cheryl that existed before she became so tired and jaded with others people's lies that she built some wall around her heart and worked out some crazy guidelines that were supposed to keep her from getting hurt again. Don't make me out to be the bad guy here, Cheryl, when all I want to do is love you."

"You're not the bad guy," Cheryl responded, struggling with her emotions. "You're the good guy here, Noah, and that's what scares me the most. I'm finally in control again. After two long hard years I know who I am and exactly where I'm going." She gave a soft laugh. "At least, I did until the people in Turning Point started giving me directions. Noah, I swore I'd never set myself up for a fall again. That if ever I fell in love, if ever someone came along, then it would be on my terms. I've done the running around, supporting someone to follow his dreams, and I vowed that next time I'd want someone to help me follow mine. Then you came along." He pulled her toward him then, his arms wrapping fiercely around her as if he couldn't bear to let her go. She rested her head on his chest. "Even though I didn't know my own name, you made me feel safe, Noah, that there was nothing to worry about. Magic did happen. I wasn't just put here to help you with Beth, I was put here to find you. And the easiest thing in the world would be for me to follow my heart, to say to hell with it, what have I got to lose by staying?"

"What *have* you got to lose?" Noah asked gently, closing his eyes.

"The only piece of me that's left."

He never got to respond. A shrill *bleep* from Beth's cell phone made them both jump. "There's a signal," she exclaimed.

For a second, neither of them moved.

"I'd better let Mitch know that you're safe, arrange Beth's transfer." Noah's eyes held hers. "What do I tell him, Cheryl?"

For a second she wavered, reluctant to leave this world they'd created, no matter how fraught with danger— both physical and emotional danger—it had become.

"Tell Mitch that I'm ready to come back to work," Cheryl said at last.

"You're sure?"

Slowly she nodded, her heart stilling as he punched in some numbers. The wait for Mitch to pick up seemed interminable. At last he did, and Cheryl listened as Noah summed up the roller coaster they had ridden for the past thirty-six hours in a few short sentences.

"They'll be here at first light." Noah's voice was flat as he handed her the phone. "Earlier if the roads clear, but if not, they'll send in a chopper. I told him Beth needed further surgery, and she's right up there on the list of evacuees, but they're still working flat out. It seems they've had a helluva time. Mitch wants to talk to you."

Slowly Cheryl took the phone, and somehow hearing Mitch's voice made her aware of the tension that had been holding her together. Tears slid down her cheeks as Mitch told her how glad he was that she was still around.

"I thought we'd lost you there, Cheryl."

"I'm sorry." Her words were strangled as she clutched the telephone. "Sorry for giving everyone such a fright, and I'm so sorry about your Jeep."

"It's a Jeep, Cheryl. After the night we've all had, it kind of puts things in perspective, doesn't it."

She couldn't answer, just nodded into the phone.

"And don't even think about working."

"What about…" Cheryl began, but Mitch answered before she finished.

"We've got everything covered. They breed 'em tough out here, Cheryl. I'm just glad that you're okay. Really glad," he added softly.

"What about Jolene?" Wiping her tear-streaked cheek with the back of her hand Cheryl remembered that Mitch had sent his daughter out on a call before the hurricane struck. She held her breath, waiting for a happy ending, for Mitch to laugh and tell her Jolene was fine.

It never came.

"She's a tough one." Mitch swallowed. "She'll be okay."

"Mitch…" Cheryl's sob was genuine but unheeded.

"She'll be okay," he said again firmly. "You came back to us, didn't you, so why shouldn't Jolene?"

Cheryl could feel Noah's arms around her. He took the phone from her, ending the conversation with practical details, then heading over to her on the sofa.

"Jolene's still out there," she said.

Noah didn't say anything. He didn't tell her that Jolene wasn't the only one missing. From what Mitch had said, even after the hell of yesterday, Turning Point was again facing one of its darkest nights. But Noah knew she couldn't take that now. Tonight was for being strong, for being positive, for holding on to each other and holding the dream just a little bit longer. Noah knew Cheryl's inner reserves had been dredged till they were dry, and he needed to be strong for them no matter how much he was bleeding inside.

"Mitch said not to think about working."

"He's right," Noah agreed. "You swallowed half a river, Cheryl. You've got a row of stitches in your cheek and you look like you've done ten rounds with Mike Tyson. You need to see a doctor, rest in your own bed. You need peace."

"It's over, isn't it." Her voice was hollow. The briefest of conversations with Mitch had rendered her both physically and emotionally exhausted.

Noah shook his head, reaching out into the darkness for her.

"It isn't over, Cheryl. We've still got tonight."

CHAPTER TWELVE

"DO YOU THINK he's okay?" She was hanging over the sofa, gazing at the sleeping infant in the drawer, scarcely able to believe he could have come through a day like today so unscathed, so utterly oblivious, and now be so peacefully asleep.

Sleeping wasn't even on the agenda for Noah and Cheryl. Both knew their time together was precious, that the hours that lay before them were numbered, and they had decided that resting could come later, that right here, right now they would simply enjoy the moment, push the past and future aside and cram as much as they could into the time that was left. It seemed wrong somehow to make love with Paul in the room, but it was nice just to lie there, to hold each other.

Reassured that the baby was fine, Cheryl rested her head back on Noah's chest and laughed into the darkness as a lazy hand stroked her bare arm. They'd been comparing the worlds of a laid-back veterinarian and an uptight nurse.

"You really have a daily schedule?" Noah asked, and Cheryl felt his laughter beneath her cheek.

She playfully thumped him to be quiet, but Noah wasn't about to let it go.

"You're telling me you make a list each night for the following day? That you plan your meals a week in advance."

"I have a weekly list," Cheryl corrected. "I just *update* it in the evening."

"Why?"

"I work shifts." Propping herself up on her elbow, she managed a laugh at her own expense. "I just like to be organized, fit everything in."

"Like what?"

"Well…" She pondered the question. "I belong to a gym, and if I'm on the late shift, I try to work out around ten a.m., but if I'm on a morning shift, I go to the hospital gym after I'm done at work. I'm pretty tired by then. The last thing I want to do is open the fridge and find there's nothing for dinner. Believe me, in the emergency room there aren't any grateful patents waving casseroles and chicken soup—"

"Maybe we should move him by the wall," Cheryl suggested as Noah climbed over her and peered into the homemade crib, somehow managing to massage her shoulder at the same time.

"Why?"

"In case we forget he's there. In case you get up in the night to go to the…"

"Cheryl, your obsessive-compulsive disorder is so misplaced here. You're with a guy who at any given time has either a laboring puppy or newborn kittens on the floor. My feet don't touch the ground until I've turned on the lights."

"I guess." Cheryl sighed as Noah eased back down onto the deliciously cramped sofa. "It's just that he's so tiny."

"Makes you feel sort of grown-up, doesn't it?" His voice was still light but his tone more serious as she rose up on her elbow again, watching him through smiling eyes. "I know I joke and everything, but it's not just a kitten or a puppy or Georgina. I mean, it's a real little person lying there."

"Who's got a mom that needs to be checked on."

"I'll go," Noah offered, even though it should have been Cheryl's turn. "You gave a lot of blood today, Cheryl, and you're coughing. You really should be resting."

"I'll rest on the plane home," Cheryl answered. "I really want to see how Beth's doing. Anyway, you're talking to a health freak, remember? I'll whip up another high-protein, multivitamin smoothie when I get up in the morning and I'll soon be as good as new."

She slipped out of the blanket and stood for a moment. "It's nearly midnight. I should give her something to eat and drink and then have her nil orally. They'll be operating as soon as she gets there."

"Just something light," Noah agreed, watching as she tossed her long mane behind her. "And maybe bring another bottle up for his lordship. For a little guy, he sure eats a lot."

Being with Noah felt so right. Barely two days ago she hadn't even known he existed.

Yet here she was, standing in a drafty kitchen in the

middle of the night in Noah's socks and surgical blues, with the dogs lying in their basket.

She smiled as she poured formula into a baby bottle, and for a decadent moment she let her mind wander. She imagined that Madge and Buster were a permanent fixture in her life, that it was Noah and her baby she was preparing a bottle for, that this wasn't one stolen night never to be repeated, and that Noah was waiting for her upstairs just as he always did, and always would.

It hurt.

It felt so right to be here that it actually hurt.

"HEY."

Beth was rubbing her eyes, blinking as Cheryl flicked on the side light. "I brought you some tea and toast."

"It's midnight," Beth groaned, straining to read the alarm clock.

"I know, but they'll be operating on you as soon as you get to Houston, so now's your last chance for a pig-out."

"A midnight feast." Beth smiled sleepily as Cheryl plumped the pillows and helped her sit up, careful not to disturb Flynn. "I hope you're going to help me with all this."

"The coffee's mine," Cheryl grinned, picking up a triangle of toast and nibbling the edges. "I've just given Noah a bottle and a hand towel, so I'll hide in here for a bit while he figures out how to change Paul."

"I need to feed him."

"Not now, Beth," Cheryl said. "You're on strong

painkillers and antibiotics, and you're still a bit dehydrated. Let Noah give him another bottle tonight."

"My breasts hurt."

"Here." An empty glass wasn't ideal but Cheryl helped Beth to express some milk and alleviate the pain of her engorged breasts. The small but intimate act seemed to bring the two women closer.

"Hal's never changed him." Beth shook her head. "Not that he doesn't want to, of course. It's just I…"

"Do it better?" Cheryl ventured. As the other woman nodded, Cheryl noticed for the first time how young Beth was, and how pretty. It struck Cheryl that even though they had shared so much, they actually knew very little about each other.

"How old are you, Beth?"

"Twenty-five. I look older, I know…."

"You don't," Cheryl said. "I guess with Flynn being seven and everything, I just figured you were older."

"I was only eighteen when I had Flynn." Beth fiddled with her toast for a moment, pushing it around the plate, then slowly opened up. "Mom and Dad live out at Corpus Christi. Hal's parents are good and everything, but they're…"

"Not yours."

"I wish they lived in Turning Point," Beth admitted. "Mom's really got her head together. When she's here she's always telling me I should let Hal do more for Flynn. I know it will be the same with Paul, worse probably after what happened to Cody…."

Their eyes met and Cheryl gave a nod of encouragement, understanding the momentous step it had been for Beth to include Cody so easily in a conversation.

"I want him to help—I need him to help. It's just somehow I can't let go."

"It must be hard, Beth," Cheryl said thoughtfully, treading very carefully, wishing she was more appropriately qualified to help. "You know, when I was a student and I did my stint in OB, I had this dad who wanted to bath his son and the mother was having hysterics. I was, too. You should have seen this guy—he was huge. The sight of his massive hands holding this wriggling tiny baby was nerve-racking, and he plunged him in the bath as if he was…"

"Dipping a sheep?" Beth offered, and Cheryl nodded.

"Just like that. I was about to go and step in, you know, do the supernurse bit. I could see the mother was beside herself and I didn't want her to get upset. Then the senior nurse arrived. She would have been coming up for retirement. She'd spent her whole working life in OB and knew everything. This was a woman who could get the most fretful baby off to sleep just by wrapping him up properly. Anyway, she said that if we interfered now, if we told this guy he was doing it wrong, this would be the first and last bath he gave that baby. And you know what?" She looked at Beth's expectant face and smiled.

"The baby survived the 'sheep dip,' and even had a fresh diaper and gown put on. The gown was back to front, but the baby didn't seem to mind. That little guy would be eleven years old now, and I bet his dad changed half his diapers and gave him his bath each night when he was small.

"Babies are tough, Beth. Look at what Paul's been through today, and the little fella's fine. It's no wonder you're overly anxious after what happened to Cody. There's nothing wrong in admitting you need help to get through being a mother to a new baby again."

"I know," Beth admitted. "I know you're right. I've been lying here thinking about it, and even though I wish this accident hadn't happened, maybe it was just meant to be. Maybe this is what I need. I'm going to get help, Cheryl. The second I come to from the operation, I'm going to ask for someone to come and talk to me. What Hal and Flynn and I have got—it's just too good to let it slip away when there's help out there."

"I'm proud of you," Cheryl offered, and even if it sounded a bit corny, it was heartfelt. "So proud of you, Beth."

"Can I have Paul in with me? I'll honestly sleep better if he's beside me, and the second he wakes, I'll send Flynn to come and get you."

Cheryl hesitated for a second, but Beth needed her boys near. "When he's had his bottle and been changed, I'll bring him in beside you. But in the meantime, I want you to try to get some rest."

"Wish you were here." Beth smiled sleepily. "I wish there was someone like you in Turning Point who could actually point us in the right direction."

WHEN CHERYL WALKED into the living room, she saw Noah silhouetted against the window, the baby cradled in his arms like a football. Hearing her enter, he pressed a finger to his lips, indicating for her to be quiet.

Making her way over to the sofa, she climbed beneath the blanket and lay back on the cushions simply watching. The moon provided enough light through the taped-up window that she could see the silhouette of his dark torso. His muscular arms cradled the infant, his hair flopping forward as he stared down at the baby. Cheryl felt a lump in her throat. Everything she wanted was there for the taking if only she could summon the courage to say yes. For two years she'd vowed that if love ever came along again it would be on her terms, that her career would always be her mainstay. Yet here she was, a mere whisper away from throwing caution to the wind and allowing herself to be caught up in the dream that was Noah Arkin.

"Penny for them." Making his way over, Noah sat on the sofa beside her. Paul was making sweet baby sounds as he dreamed his milky dreams, and she saw Noah's soft smile, felt the warmth of his gaze.

"I'm just thinking that I wish this night would never end."

He gave a slow nod, understanding blazing in his eyes.

"Beth wants Paul in with her." Cheryl's fingers brushed the baby's soft cheeks. "I said that once he was settled I'd bring him in."

Noah nodded, staring down at the infant's face, an expression she couldn't read in his eyes. "Poor Cody." He was looking back at Paul now, and when he spoke, his voice was low and thoughtful. "I'll never forget that day as long as I live."

"It must have been awful."

He nodded. "I knew then why I was a vet, Cheryl, and not a doctor. I couldn't go through that again and live to tell the tale. I honestly don't know how you do it. Doesn't it get to you?"

"Oh, it gets to me." Cheryl let out a weary sigh. "And anyone who says that it doesn't is either lying or so completely burnt out that they don't know what's real anymore. But I guess at the end of the day, you just pray the good will outweigh the bad, and you console yourself that you save more lives than you lose."

"It doesn't put you off having kids?"

She shook her head.

"It did me."

"You've just never met Ms. Right...." Cheryl mentally kicked herself and wished she could somehow take the words back. This sort of talk wasn't going to get her anywhere. "I'd better get him back to Beth."

"I'll do it," Noah offered, levering himself off the sofa and carefully placing the baby back into the crib. "She'll probably rest better with both her boys beside her."

Beth would rest easier with two of the people she loved most around her. Cheryl knew that. It was the same for her with Noah. The few hours they had been together felt so perfect, as if this was how life was supposed to be.

Would the fights that had crept up on her and Joe have happened if it had been her and Noah?

For the first time in her adult life, Cheryl didn't automatically fold her clothes after she slipped them off. She just dropped the garments onto the floor as she pondered her conundrum.

No, the fights wouldn't have happened, she decided.

Because no matter how she played it, no matter how she tried to imagine Noah as a twentysomething student, somehow she knew that despite his focus, despite his inner desire to succeed in his chosen field, it wouldn't have been at the expense of her happiness. There was nothing remotely selfish about the man who was now crossing the room toward her, unself-consciously discarding his clothes, disarming her with a seductive smile before pulling back the crumpled blankets and climbing in beside her. His body was cool, and he drew warmth from her as he eased alongside her. And though the desire was there, the urgency was gone, allowing time for a more languid discovery.

He was like an open book.

Which didn't mean predictable, Cheryl mused as he ran a strong hand down the length of her side, capturing the hollow of her waist and the curve of her hip as she turned to face him. He was the kind of book where you glimpsed a page and just knew you wanted to go on—to turn the pages and find out the secrets within.

So why couldn't she stay?

"Just us two," he whispered.

"Just us," she breathed back, running a lazy finger around his nipple, feeling the swell of his manhood nudging her thigh. His hand was still working its magic,

but was more insistent now, massaging the soft marsh-
mallow of her inner thighs as his lips found hers, kissing the hollows of her throat with a reverence that made
her dizzy. Her hand crept to his back, feeling the taut
muscles beneath her splayed fingers as his lips left hers.
He blazed a trail of hot kisses along her throat, and each
flick of his tongue had her sinking deeper into the moment. Her head arched back as he worked his way down
to her breasts, teasing her with featherlight kisses. One
hand was now stroking the soft down between her
thighs, the teasing upward strokes light, yet finely at-
tuned to her needs. She was torn between frustration and
exhilaration, wanting so much to reciprocate, to feel
him in her hands, to taste him with her mouth. Yet she
was paralyzed with pleasure, content simply to lie there
and let him take control.

"I'm going to take you to places you've never been,"
he promised, his husky drawl doing the strangest things
to her. "I'm going to give you some loving that you'll
never forget."

He suckled the sweet pale flesh of her breast as his fingers worked on, and before she could beg him to end this
delicious torture, she could feel the distant thrum of her
orgasm. Her thighs taut, her pelvis tilting toward him, she
uttered low moans of wonder, as he took her ever higher.
The intensity of her orgasm was so overwhelming, she
lay there spent and exhausted as the tremors abated. But
when she felt his arousal nudging her trembling thighs
apart, slipping inside her sweet warmth, there was nothing to do but wrap her legs around him and pull him

deeper inside, scarcely able to comprehend that the shuddering train of her roller coaster hadn't yet come to a halt.

Noah called her name as he exploded within her, and she came again, clinging to his muscular back. And this time her eyes were open, and so were Noah's, both capturing the overwhelming beauty of the moment. The terror and ecstasy of the last thirty-six hours had all been condensed and suddenly released. Tears of pain and joy coursed down her cheeks, followed by exhausted, exhilarated sobs that needed no explanation as he held her, loved her, adored her.

For the last time.

CHAPTER THIRTEEN

TIME HAD NO MEANING NOW. It was almost impossible to comprehend that so much could happen in thirty-six hours. Nearly drowning. Being saved. Beth's accident. Falling in love....

It was as if the world had been put on pause since Noah had pulled her from the river, minutes ticking away like hours, giving them plenty of time to get to know each other, enough time to cement the attraction that had been there from the first time they set eyes on each other.

But now God, or the powers that be, had clearly decided to get things moving. The darkness that had bathed them receded at an alarming rate. Gray fingers of dawn crept through the room. Birds that should surely stay quiet for an hour or so longer sang the dawn chorus with a gusto that under any other circumstances would have been beautiful.

"Stay."

Even though she was facing away from him, Cheryl had known he wasn't asleep. "I want to," she admitted.

"But?" Noah asked, because clearly there was one.

"Please, Noah." She shook her head, determined not

to let him see her tears, knowing this was as hard on him as it was on her.

Harder perhaps.

Noah didn't have any doubts. He seemed to have enough faith in their relationship for both of them, it was she who was torn with indecision, she, who for the first time in her adult life had no idea what to do.

"Even when Joe left, and when my parents broke up, I knew I'd be okay." She lay silent for a moment, gripped with the same piercing grief that had swamped her at the end of her marriage. And even though it had been two full years, still she managed total recall of horrible, aching emptiness, the thudding disappointment that all the hope and love that had filled them at the start simply hadn't been enough. "But as bad as it was, as awful as I felt there for a while, I had my work, Noah, and I had my pride. Even though I'd lost everything, I still had that little piece of me that no one could take away. No one, that is, except…" Turning, she looked up at him. "Except you, Noah." He didn't answer, just stared back at her as she asked the most difficult question of all. "Would you do it for me?"

She blinked at him in the dim morning light, taking in every flicker of his reaction. "I'm not asking you to hop on a plane tomorrow, but if things did work out between us, could you ever see yourself selling your practice and heading to California to set up shop in Courage Bay?"

She didn't want him to answer, didn't want to hear him say it, but the silence that hung between them was even worse somehow.

"Cheryl…"

"Don't." Slipping out from under the blanket, she sat for a moment on the edge of the sofa, running a trembling hand through her long dark hair before turning her confused eyes to his. "Don't try to sweeten it, Noah, because we both know the answer."

"You're not being fair, Cheryl. I've got a life here now, a career. I'm the only vet for miles. I can't just walk away. You've been in Courage Bay two years, your family lives in—"

"It's still my home," Cheryl broke in. "It's still my life I'd be upending, and the bottom line is that you wouldn't do it for me."

"So that's it, then." His voice was raw, and her pain was so raw she couldn't bring herself to look at him as he spoke. "You set me some impossible test, and when I don't measure up, you walk away."

"It's not impossible, Noah. What I'm asking you to do is no more than you'd be asking from me."

She pulled on her clothes. It was easier to be angry than admit to feeling the chasm of despair where her soul used to be.

"I'm going to get Beth and the boys ready…."

"Don't go, Cheryl."

A strong hand gripped her wrist, attempting to pull her back down onto their bed, but she shook him off, knowing one look, one touch and she would break down.

"Stay and talk."

"There's no point." Heading for the door, she didn't even turn around.

THE ATMOSPHERE was so tense in the house that she escaped to the shed and stood staring at the piglets' wagging tails, her eyes so dry she couldn't squeeze out a single tear.

"They're on their way." Noah was in the doorway, standing hesitant and unsure, but Buster had no such reserve. Slipping between Noah's legs, she headed toward her mistress. Noah walked over more slowly. "I brought you these." He handed her some clothing. "Just some old jeans and a sweater I shrunk in the wash. Figured you'd be more comfortable traveling in them."

"I can only see eleven." Gesturing to the baby pigs, she sniffed rather ungraciously, her eyes scanning the straw for the one that was missing.

"Yeah, it died," Noah said in a matter-of-fact voice, then changed tack when he saw her face crumple. "Cheryl, it happens all the time. The mother overlays them, or they're the runt. It's just the way it is…."

He was trying to help, trying to say the right thing, but each word only wounded her further. God, why did everything have to make her cry? Accepting a tissue, she blew her nose loudly, then sniffed again. She managed a wobbly smile when finally she faced him.

"I'm doing you a favor, really," she said.

"How did you work that one out?"

"Aren't vets' wives supposed to be salt-of-the-earth types?" Cheryl sniffed. "Rosy cheeks and practical natures? I'd never let you sell any of the piglets. We'd be overrun with eleven more Mabels. The dogs and Georgina would all be sporting pink bows. I'd ignore all your food charts, sneak Georgina chocolate…."

"Sounds good to me."

She could hear the *thud-thud* of choppers in the distance, and it was almost a relief when Noah pushed open the massive rolling door. Buster whimpered in her arms, knowing something was up and begging for reassurance. But all Cheryl could do was cling to the short clipped fur, feel the solid weight of the little body in her arms and wish things didn't have to be this way. They watched as the giant black bird swooped out of the sky, the trees bending beneath the power of the false wind the rotors created.

"Mitch is here, too!"

The surprise was evident in Noah's voice, and Cheryl managed to lift herself out of her gloom long enough to head over. A fire department vehicle pulled up near the helicopter.

"The road must have cleared," he concluded.

"Who's the other guy?" Cheryl asked, mentally answering her own question as she registered the man's pale, anxious face. He jumped out of the truck and ducked his head before running under the blades toward the house. "Hal?"

Noah nodded. "I'd better go and talk to him. You get dressed, I'll meet you outside."

He greeted the worried husband as Cheryl darted into the clinic bathroom to change, then wandered around, silently bidding goodbye to everything that had become familiar. She felt Buster's cold nose against her hot tear-streaked cheeks, the worried whimpers matching her own feelings, and as she stroked the dog, soothed her, the whimpers faded, and Cheryl wished her own problems and fears could so easily be erased.

"Hey."

The voice was reassuringly familiar, so much so that a fresh batch of tears pricked her eyes. Seeing the rough, knowing face of Mitch Kannon standing by the fire truck, Cheryl felt her resolve crumble. He wasn't a fire chief all of a sudden, wasn't a tough, assured emergency worker. He was more like a father figure who really seemed to understand what she'd been through. Coming over to Cheryl, he held her for a moment.

And Cheryl wasn't the only one struggling with emotions. Appalled at her fragility, Mitch gripped her in a bear hug, obviously stunned that the brittle, confident woman he had sent out on the easiest job had suffered so much, that the proud, good-looking New Yorker he had waved off was like a fragile child in his arms, an angry scar over her cheek and a flood of pain in her heart.

"I'm sorry about the Jeep, sorry that I wasn't there to help when the storm hit...."

"We managed," Mitch said gruffly, "and I don't want to hear another damn word about the Jeep. It's a hunk of metal, Cheryl. Don't give it another thought. You're safe." His voice was thick. "I tried to tell you to get off the bridge, Cheryl. I was screaming into my phone for you to back off, but there was so much static on the line that I knew you couldn't hear me. Then all of a sudden

the line cleared, and all I could hear was you screaming. I thought we'd lost you, Cheryl. I thought for sure
you'd drowned. I radioed through for a vehicle to head
straight down there, and when they radioed back and
said the bridge was down…"

"I can come back and work," Cheryl offered, but
Mitch immediately shook his head.

"You're in no fit state to work. You're on the first
flight out of here."

As if in response, she gave a moist cough and struggled to catch her breath. Mitch eyed her in concern, and
suddenly home sounded good to Cheryl; the cool, white
emptiness of her apartment, the order of the life she had
created for herself in Courage Bay.

Mitch was right; home was where she needed to be.
And yet…

Forcibly she pushed her misgivings aside as Beth was
stretchered across the grass by an efficient emergency
retrieval team. Cheryl knew then that her time was up,
and she sought out Noah, scarcely able to believe he
hadn't come out to say goodbye. Mitch would be too
busy to linger once Beth and Paul were safely boarded
onto the helicopter.

"I don't know how to thank you," Beth said as Cheryl
approached the stretcher and gave Beth's good hand a
squeeze, "and how sorry I am for what happened."

"It wasn't your fault," Cheryl said. "It was an accident."

"Even so, you could have—"

"Don't," Cheryl broke in. "I'm fine, and you will be
soon. Don't linger on the whys and what-ifs."

"You'll be telling me soon that this was for the best, that one day we'll look back on all this and be glad it happened."

"Maybe." Cheryl smiled bravely, but her heart wasn't in it. Even with all that she'd found here in Turning Point, it surely couldn't cancel out the raw ache she was destined to lug around for the rest of her life—the pain of Noah's rejection.

And it *was* a rejection.

He wouldn't move to Courage Bay for her, and no amount of shuffling facts changed the final score.

Give up on her career for a man?

Been there, done that, Cheryl thought ruefully.

And though Noah was a million light years from Joe, the equation was the same, and she had promised herself that she would never put herself in that situation again.

"How do you do it?" Noah was beside her, trying to smile. "You're the only woman I've met who could sex up an old pair of jeans and a baggy black sweater." He gave up trying to keep the moment light, and she watched as he swallowed hard, then dragged in a breath before talking again. "I brought a couple of your fans along to say goodbye."

And there was Georgina, shivering beside him. The horse looked old and tired, and Cheryl realized she wasn't the only one the storm had emotionally and physically battered.

"Hey, little lady." Putting Buster down next to Madge, Cheryl cuddled the soft chestnut-colored fur and ran a gentle hand over the horse's long proud face. "It's over, Georgina, you're safe now." Concerned, Cheryl turned to Noah. "She doesn't seem well."

"She's tired, Cheryl," Noah replied. "Tired and old and very sick."

"It's the same with her mistress." Mitch Kannon's voice was grim. "We evacuated Mary last night. She had a heart attack. It doesn't look good."

"What will happen to Georgina?" Cheryl swallowed hard. "I mean, if her owner doesn't make it. She won't have to be destroyed, will she?"

Noah shook his head, but Cheryl's relief was short-lived. "I'd be happy to have you, wouldn't I, girl?" Noah said softly, but his voice was hollow with sadness. "But if Mary goes, I've a feeling Georgina won't be too far behind."

"Best get on." Mitch was shaking Noah's hand now as Buster flung himself at Cheryl.

Even though dogs didn't cry, she could have sworn there were tears in those confused black eyes as Buster howled without shame, yelped and nipped as Noah prized her off.

"She's going to miss you," Noah said gruffly. "We're all going to miss you."

"I'm sorry." Cheryl's teeth were chattering so violently she could barely get the words out.

"You've got nothing to be sorry for," Noah said.

But Cheryl pushed on, refusing his comfort. "I should never have said I was free to love you when I didn't know the truth."

"You have to think of yourself first, Cheryl, and as much as it hurts, I do understand. I'm sorry, too," he added sadly. "Sorry that I can't just walk away from my life, that I can't—"

Mitch was tooting the horn, oblivious to all that had taken place. This wasn't a casual farewell, but even if he had known, it wouldn't make a difference. There was no time in his busy schedule for long goodbyes. Not when there was a town to take care of.

"I have to go," Cheryl said, but she couldn't move her legs.

"I'll…" Noah started to say, but Cheryl shook her head fiercely.

"Let's not make promises neither of us is prepared to keep, Noah. Our time together was special, magical, wonderful, but I'm not up to long-distance love, I need more than a phone call or an e-mail to sustain me."

"Remember Alexis and Ewa," Noah reminded her, wiping her tears away with his hands. "The whole world was against them, but still they came through."

"It was a nice story." Cheryl gave a watery smile. "But it belongs in the past, Noah."

It was only a few steps to the fire department vehicle, but she felt as if she were walking the plank. It took an almost inhuman physical effort just to haul herself into the truck, and, unlike for Georgina, no amount of chocolate would have made leaving easier. She was walking away from the best thing to ever happen to her, and she couldn't bring herself to turn for one final wave.

"Let's get you home," Mitch said.

That sounded nice, but right now Cheryl truly didn't know what home meant.

CHAPTER FOURTEEN

IT HAD NEVER FELT SO empty before.

The home he'd built from the ground, the home that had comforted him no matter how bad a day he'd had, suddenly felt empty.

Now that the roads were open, a massive influx of patients had arrived at the clinic. Ranchers were calling in, asking Noah to come out and check the animals that were their livelihood. And then there were the repairs to Noah's property. Upstairs had been completely gutted by the storm and he was confined to the lower floor of his home and the clinic, but in comparison to some folks, he knew he really had nothing to complain about. Plenty of things to keep Noah busy, plenty of reasons to work himself into the ground. And still he managed to head to town and help Mitch. It got him through from five in the morning until midnight, when if he was really lucky, all that was left to do was his last round of good-nights before feeding Buster and Madge.

Oh, and himself.

Suddenly that chicken soup didn't taste quite so wonderful anymore, and the casseroles were more effort than they were worth.

"Come on, Buster." Noah watched as the little mutt halfheartedly nudged the tray of food he had put down for her. He broke off a piece of dog biscuit and tossed it to her, but she nudged it away, those bright eyes uninterested now. "You really think that starving yourself is going to bring her home? She's a California girl, Buster. She'd admire your willpower and no doubt mix you up one of her smoothies, then have you pound the sidewalk...." Even Noah didn't appreciate his own humor. And Buster wasn't the only one off her food. Three nights in a row Noah had shoveled his microwaved meal around the plate, stared at a pile of blurry figures on his computer, even watched the late-night shopping channel—anything to stave off going to bed alone.

Three nights in a row he'd dialed her phone number. Not even an answering machine picked up. He'd listened to the endless ringing, willing Cheryl to pick up just so he could hear that voice once more. He could just picture her staring at the call display, knowing it was him phoning and waiting for the ringing to end, or coming in from a shift and seeing his area code displayed.

Noah Schmuck Arkin.

Noah Schmuck Arkin, who had let the best thing that had ever happened to him simply walk out of his life.

It would be written on his gravestone.

"Come on." Whistling to Madge, he indicated the door. "Let's go and meet the trees, then call it a night."

But even the normally much-awaited, late-night walk didn't fire up Buster or Madge. Lethargy was clearly the order of the day.

"Hey, guys, why don't you try to summon up some enthusiasm while I go and check next door."

Flicking on the lights, he worked his way around the clinic, giving out the midnight antibiotics, updating his charts and running a set of obs on his two post-op patients, but just as he went to turn off the lights and take Madge and Buster out, he paused a moment and stared into the cage where a proud, tired lady lay.

"Hey, Georgina." Long eyelashes fluttered back at him, and if it had been a pink shawl and not a pile of sawdust she was lying on, he'd have sworn she'd pulled it closer around her shoulders. "How are you doing?"

Her owner had died; the call had come through around 6:00 p.m. that Mary had passed away, but Noah hadn't had the heart to break it to the old horse.

Which was stupid, Noah reasoned. As if Georgina was going to understand what he said. But still he couldn't bring himself to say the words, to tell Georgina that her mistress wasn't ever coming home.

"You know anyway, don't you, girl," Noah said softly, looking into her eyes, then reaching for a stethoscope and listening to her old heart.

Even though he loved animals, in some instances more than people, Noah wasn't overly sentimental where they were concerned, unless it was one of his own pets. There was a kind of mental subclause there for Madge and the multitude of dogs who had come before her. Oh, and Mabel, as well. But in much the same way doctors and nurses probably coped with human patients, Noah held back. Sure it hurt, and sure you felt people's losses, but if you were going to survive, you couldn't get too attached. Death was part and parcel of a day's work in this game.

"Sleep tight, Georgina." Noah gave her a final stroke before closing the cage door. A sadness filled him when Georgina didn't even try to fight back, didn't whinny in protest or try to nip his hand as he shot the bolt. She just stared at her keeper with sad, dark eyes.

Maybe it was because Georgina *thought* she was human, or maybe it was because her beloved owner had died today, but as he turned to go, Noah knew he would be back. After walking around the clinic with Buster and Madge, for once obediently at his heels, Noah lifted Georgina out of her cage and led her into the living room of the house. The real reason he was doing this, of course, was Cheryl. A special lady who had had the foresight and the compassion to bring the frightened animal out of the clinic and into the adjoining bedroom, and Noah knew that if Cheryl were still here, she'd insist on it now.

Noah took the dogs for a very quick trip outside again, then returned to the house to be with Georgina.

"Maybe we should forget the diet." He smiled, breaking open a bar of chocolate and giving her a piece, before stretching out on the sofa. Buster lay shivering by the door, obviously still hoping that Cheryl would magically appear.

"Come on, girl," Noah called, but he knew it was useless. She'd stay there waiting all night. Madge circled around on his stomach before planting herself firmly at his feet as Noah flicked off the lamp. Reaching over the side of the couch, he idly stroked the miniature horse, listening to her ragged breaths, the endless ticking of the clock, wishing for the practical demands of the morning. He fought an impulse to phone Cheryl again in the hope that maybe, just maybe, this time she'd pick up, let him plead his case once more. Hell, he'd settle for a few sharp words.

If only it meant he heard her voice.

THEY WANTED to admit her!

Admit her for rest and IV antibiotics, and Cheryl couldn't even argue the point. Well, she tried, but given that the examining doctor was the chief of emergency, she didn't get very far. The more Cheryl argued, the more Rachel pushed to admit her.

Why couldn't it have been some first-year attendant checking over her X rays? Oh, no, because she was one of their own, because it was Trauma Nurse Cheryl Tierney, who had been flown in from Texas with a raging fever and a cough, Rachel simply couldn't stop. Cheryl had been told in no uncertain terms that for the foreseeable future she could forget work, forget the gym, forget her whole routine, in fact. A couple of nights in the hospital and a full week of downtime was ordered, and then, if she improved, Rachel would think about letting her back to work.

"I've got a slight cough." Cheryl slumped back on the hospital gurney, mortified at being dressed in a lemon-yellow gown and wheeled by a porter to X ray through

her own department. She'd felt okay in Turning Point—
aside from a broken heart—not great, but okay. But as
soon as the airplane had lifted into the sky, whether it
was the decompression or just the end of an exhausting
journey, her body had simply given out on her. Her
cough became more rasping, every joint in her body
ached, her cheeks flushed with fever, and she was barely
able to walk the short distance from the plane to a waiting wheelchair. Then, horror of horrors, she was driven
by ambulance into her own department. "There's no
reason I can't have some oral antibiotics and come back
to work in a couple of days."

"You've got a patch of consolidation on the right
lower lobe." Rachel pointed at the X ray on the view-
finder. "Which, if I'm not mistaken, is pneumonia, or
do you know something I don't?"

Slinking farther down on the pillow, Cheryl mut-
tered something rather ungracious.

"You're not in the trauma room now, Cheryl," Rachel
reminded her, "so lose the attitude, okay? For now
you're a patient, *my* patient, and if I get even an inkling
that you're not going to comply with my orders, I'll sign
you off work for a full month and tell the admitting phy-
sician that you're noncompliant and maybe a five-day
admission might be more appropriate." She eyed the
X ray film more closely. "Which might not be such a
bad idea, in fact. I thought you'd at least have a couple
of broken ribs, given the extent of the bruising. I guess
those multivitamins you swear by must have some merit
after all." She paused.

"You're in a bad way, Cheryl." Rachel's expression was kind but firm. "You're covered in bruises, and you've got a tender rib cage, which as you well know makes deep breathing more difficult. Over the next few days, as the bruises come out, you're going to feel worse, not better. On top of all that you gave blood." She paused for a moment, watching as Cheryl swallowed hard. "Cheryl, I don't say this sort of thing lightly, so know that I mean it. You have my support in all this—you were sent to do a job and you did it well. You're trained to make tough calls, and no matter how much the powers that be try, not every scenario can be covered in a policy book or summed up in a pile of legal jargon. We're here to save lives, Cheryl, and that's what you did. I'm going to have to speak to the hospital's legal team, and no doubt they'll want a full statement from you, but from what you've told me, it was either a case of sit back and watch her die or…"

"Give blood and scrub in for a veterinarian?"

"Hopefully the hospital solicitor will put it a bit more eloquently," Rachel said, "but in a word, yes. Now, with all you've been through, it's no wonder you're not well. And if you don't do this right, if you don't follow my orders to the letter, you're going to end up with full-blown pneumonia and at least a week's admission, followed by a couple of weeks of rehab."

"Okay, I'll rest," Cheryl said rather more graciously, "but I can do that at home, Rachel. I just want to be around my own things, in my own bed." Her voice trailed off, tears pricking her eyes. Appalled at the prospect of breaking down in front of her new boss, Cheryl bit down hard on her lip.

"Let me admit you for a couple of days," Rachel urged her. "Cheryl, you're not well, and it's not just the bruises or the pneumonia. I'm really worried about you." Rachel handed her a tissue and Cheryl took it gratefully. "This is a hard, tough job sometimes, and if you don't let everything out sometimes, sooner or later it catches up.

"And it's caught up with you now," she added softly, watching as Cheryl gave a reluctant nod. "You're not just physically exhausted, you're emotionally drained, too. That's a bad combination. You can pound the gym, drink your smoothies, take your multivitamins and ginseng or whatever those bullets you swallow are, but if a body's run-down and you don't stop and rest and let the world wash over you every now and then, your immune system can't keep up. Infections are serious, Cheryl. You know that. They hit you when you're down. Who's going to be at home to look after you? Who's going to cook for you and make sure you're getting enough fluids?"

"No one." It was the loneliest admission she'd ever made.

"You've got a serious infection brewing, Cheryl…." Rachel halted as a frown crossed Cheryl's face. "What is it?"

"Beth, the patient I gave the blood to—pneumonia can quickly lead to sepsis…"

"We're already on to it. I'm waiting to be put through

to one of the surgical teams in Houston, but from what you told me, the veterinarian covered her with strong antibiotics. The risk is very small."

"But there is a risk?"

"A small one, but once I let the surgeons know—" The pager was beeping in her pocket and Rachel raised an eyebrow as she looked down and turned it off. "Seems they've called back." She gave Cheryl a wink. "Houston, we may have a problem." When her joke didn't even raise a smile, Rachel patted Cheryl's hand. "I'll let them know about the infection and find out how she's doing for you, Cheryl. Do I have your permission to fax over your blood work and the results of the cultures when we get them back?"

"Of course."

It seemed forever that Cheryl lay there waiting for Rachel to return, to tell her how Beth was doing. The possible ramifications of Beth's surgery—both legal and medical—were about to make themselves known.

Rachel would stand by her. Cheryl knew that much.

And in turn she'd stand by Noah. Swear on a Bible—if it came to that—that there had been no choice. The heroic measures they had taken to save Beth's arm—Beth's life—had been the right ones....

But already it was starting.

Noah had been right when he'd said that once she left Turning Point and returned to Courage Bay she'd lose sight of the truth, lose sight of the magic, the love, the hope and confidence that had carried them through on their journey. As she lay here on a hospital gurney, staring at the equipment around her, listening to the PA system relaying messages, sending staff to where they were most needed, it was hard to fathom the desperation of the situation she and Noah had faced alone. And worse still, away from Noah, away from Turning Point, even she was beginning to have doubts about the decisions they had made….

"She's okay."

Rachel's two words ripped through her doubts.

"Better than okay," Rachel said. "She's out of surgery and they're hopeful she's going to have full function in her arm. Apparently this vet of yours did an amazing job."

"He's not *my* vet," Cheryl sniffed, but tears were starting now, the sheer horror of all she had witnessed finally catching up. "We had no choice, Rachel."

"Yes, you did." Rachel's words were firm. "And so did this vet—Noah, isn't it?"

Cheryl nodded. Just hearing his name made the impossible more real somehow.

"You could have done nothing, and there's no one who'd have blamed you. But your patient would have died, Cheryl. The surgeons in Houston have confirmed it. Her blood loss was extensive. She's having a further three units of blood transfused as we speak. Without the transfusion she wouldn't have made it, and without Noah's intervention she'd have lost her arm. He thought of everything. He covered her with penicillin cephalosporin and an aminoglycoside, which will knock any infection straight on the head. Her prognosis is good, Cheryl, and it's thanks to you and this Noah."

"Will someone let him know?" Cheryl asked. "Noah, I mean." A germ of an idea sparked in her mind. "I could call him…."

"The trauma surgeon in Houston is doing it now. He wanted to congratulate him himself. So you've got nothing to worry about except yourself. Can I go and arrange your admission?"

As if in answer, a violent spasm of coughing racked Cheryl's tired, aching body and she clutched her sore ribs. The tears she'd held in check had no option but to fall, and thankfully Rachel seemed to realize that she wanted to be left alone. Placing a box of tissues in her lap the doctor slipped out of the cubicle.

BECAUSE THE STAFF looked after their own, Cheryl was admitted to a pretty sideroom on the top floor of the hospital. From her bed she could glimpse the endless white sandy beach of Courage Bay, the pounding sapphire of the Pacific Ocean as deep and hypnotic as Noah's eyes. As she slipped between the cool sheets, an orderly placed a tray of food in front of her and a young nurse came and introduced herself as Angeline as she hooked Cheryl up to her IV antibiotics.

"I don't need to tell you how this works," she said with a smile, placing the call bell on the table beside Cheryl. "But according to the notes in Admitting, I do need to remind you that you're to use it! Apart from bathroom privileges, you're not to get out of bed, so don't think twice about pressing the call bell if you need anything." She went through the admission list effi-

ciently, only stalling when she saw the next-of-kin
Cheryl had listed. "Your mom's in New York? Is there
anyone closer we can contact if we need to?"

Cheryl shook her head. "No relatives. But the staff
downstairs in Emergency know I'm here, and I've already called my neighbor to let her know I'll be away
for a couple more days."

"Anyone else you need to call?"

For a second Cheryl's mind drifted to Noah. She
needed to talk to him, to hear his voice, to tell him
where she was, but she didn't even know his number.
She'd have to go through the operator just to get it, and
that realization spoke volumes for Cheryl.

Noah might as well be on the other side of the world.

So instead she shook her head at Angeline's offer, managing a weak smile as the nurse headed out of the room.

Lying in the pretty pastel-painted room, Cheryl
watched the antibiotics dripping in. For the first time in a
long while, she had nothing to do. No trips to the gym to
pound the treadmill, or a yoga session to supposedly relax.
No combing the shops for organic strawberries to add to
her morning smoothie, no trips to the salon for her hair,
or maybe a facial or manicure if she could find the time.

And if those rituals sounded vain, Cheryl knew they
weren't. They had more to do with order than vanity.

A semblance of control in the chaos her life had
become.

RACHEL, DAMN HER, was right, Cheryl mused as the
days dragged by, her temperature still spiking in the

early hours just to thwart her hopes of being discharged. Noah was right—Cheryl didn't let anyone close. Sure, she had friends, acquaintances, but since her parents' marriage had ended, since Joe had cheated on her, since she'd lost her husband, her lover and her childhood memories in one fell swoop, there hadn't really seemed much point in letting people in, only to have them leave.

"Hey." Angeline was back; bright and breezy, make-up immaculate as she placed a thermometer in Cheryl's ear. "Normal." She smiled. "If you can just keep that temperature of yours down tonight, you could be home tomorrow."

"Sounds good." Cheryl smiled back, and Angeline noticed.

"You look better, and I'm not just talking about your observations being normal now, you really do look better."

"I feel better," Cheryl admitted. "As much as it galled me at the time, Rachel was right to admit me. You know, I think I've been running on empty for the past six months. I've forgotten how good it feels to be rested."

"Your bruises are all gone, too," Angeline commented, listening to Cheryl's chest, then settling her back on the pillows. "Maybe I should check myself in for a few nights. I could use a bit of downtime."

"There are better ways." Cheryl grinned, but then her voice grew more serious. "Take time off if you need it, Angeline. I've been watching everyone while I'm here and I've decided that medical staff are so busy rushing around worrying about other people, they forget about themselves. We're very good at giving advice, but not so good at taking it."

"Don't do as I do, do as I say?" Angeline laughed. "That's what my father used to tell me."

"Mine, too." Cheryl smiled, and it hit her then how she never really spoke about him. Despite his faults, despite the sham of his marriage, when all was said and done, her father had been a good dad. By shutting out the pain, Cheryl realized she'd also wiped out a lot of love.

Noah had been right again.

Lying back on the pillow, she stared out the window. The waves drifted in, high tide drawing near as again her mind drifted to Noah.

"Oh, I nearly forgot." Fishing in her pocket, Angeline pulled out a piece of paper. "Dr. Sherwood, one of the first-year residents from Emergency, dropped by but you were asleep."

"Amy? Is she back at work?"

"No, she's here visiting her aunt. Apparently she's not well at all. She thought you might want to catch up. That's her cell number. She went to Turning Town as well, didn't she?"

"Turning Point," Cheryl corrected without thinking, staring at the phone number Angeline had pushed into her hand. Normally she'd have slipped it into her locker, assuming it was a duty call, but she held on to it, and when Angeline slipped out, after only a couple of moments' hesitation, Cheryl picked up the phone and decided to finally let someone in.

CHAPTER FIFTEEN

NEVER HAD IT HIT HIM like this before. Not since he was ten years old and his Labrador had died had the death of an animal affected him like this. And even though she'd been old and ready, even though he'd known it was coming, waking up and finding Georgina still and cold on the floor beside the couch had had him crying like a child. Holding the stiff body, he had wept into her chestnut-colored fur.

Another part of Cheryl was gone, too, another part of the dream lost forever.

But even though she'd left them, still he was aware of her presence. She'd brought nothing but a pile of damp muddy clothes into the house, and yet she was everywhere. He could feel her in every room, remember with exquisite, painful detail the soft contours of her skin, those guarded velvet eyes that had finally warmed him.

She was everywhere.

Long dark hairs in a comb he couldn't contemplate cleaning. The new toothbrush he had found for her still in the glass beside his. The blender still out in the clinic. Painful but blissful reminders of her.

The living room was the worst place, though—or the best, depending on how he felt.

The sofa was too big and lonely without her beside him, but sometimes in the day he'd lie there for a while. He could still smell the lingering traces of her feminine scent, imagine that proud face on the cushion beside him, the dark tumble of hair cascading around her.

And now Georgina was dead.

Another creature Cheryl had loved and left behind, gone forever now.

And somehow the incinerator didn't seem right for a lady. Noah felt Georgina deserved more. So he drove over to Mary's with Buster and Madge, and picked a few flowers from the old lady's lovingly tended garden before driving back and digging the soil, still damp from the storm, while Buster and Madge stared on forlornly.

Placing the flowers on the soft mound should have brought some closure, but instead it hurt more, allowed in more pain, more grief than Noah had thought he was capable of feeling.

He missed Cheryl.

Missed his Chocolate Girl with every fiber of his being.

"Thanks for coming."

Smiling, Amy slipped into the seat opposite Cheryl, who felt more than a little uneasy. Amy returned the smile with a slightly curious one of her own. She had every right to be confused at Cheryl's rather out-of-the-blue offer to get together for dinner once she was discharged from the hospital. They'd worked together for the better part of a year, since Amy had started her residency, but despite a mutual professional respect, the odd coffee in the staff room or an occasional moan in the change room, they weren't exactly buddies.

"So how are you doing?" Amy asked. "You look a whole lot better than when I came to see you. So when did they finally let you out?"

"Yesterday," Cheryl answered. "And yes, I do feel a whole lot better. I'll never admit it to Rachel, but a few days in bed with nothing to do except stare at the beach was exactly the right thing for the doctor to order. It was weird coming home, though." Cheryl shrugged. Her honest admission didn't come close to describing just how strange it had felt as she'd let herself in her front door. Her apartment was just as she'd left it, the answering machine half out of its box waiting to be installed, a pile of letters awaiting her attention. One in particular had made her hand shake as she read it. One more thing to deal with when she'd already been through so much. "I felt as if I'd been away for a month instead of just a few days."

"I know what you mean," Amy admitted, her voice trailing off, lost in her own world for a moment.

Cheryl fiddled with a place mat, wondering what on earth had possessed her to ask Amy to come, but she knew the answer. Even though they'd barely seen each other in Turning Point, just the simple fact that Amy had been there, could picture it in her head, somehow made Noah seem closer. It was enough for Cheryl right now.

Thankfully the rather strained silence that followed

didn't last too long. Larry, the owner of the popular diner, was always on the lookout for his regular Emergency personnel. He came over now, waving menus under their noses and chatting in his usual laid-back manner.

"How about a drink while you make your minds up, ladies," he suggested.

"A beer, thanks, Larry," Amy responded as her eyes scanned the menu. "Believe me, I've earned it."

"Sure, Amy, and how about you, Cheryl? Sparkling mineral water?"

She was about to agree to her usual, but instead she ran her eyes down the menu. "A Touch of Courage for me, thanks, Larry." Looking up, she saw Amy's slightly incredulous look. "And please don't be a doctor here and remind me that I'm on antibiotics."

"Wouldn't dream of it," Amy answered. "Actually, forget the beer, Larry. I could use a Touch of Courage myself."

"You too, huh?" Cheryl asked as Larry ambled off. "I heard your aunt is very sick. I'm sorry...."

"Thanks. But it's not just that, Cheryl...." Amy put up a hand to halt her, and Cheryl realized it was shaking.

Cheryl picked up a serviette, handed it over and sat quietly as Amy blew her nose and tried to regain control.

"They offered me a counselor at the hospital, you know," Cheryl said finally with just enough irony to bring a wobbly smile to Amy's lips.

"What did you say?"

"That they couldn't afford it. That by the time I

would have finished talking, the poor counselor would be in therapy herself."

"Hell, wasn't it?" Amy said, finally looking up. "Do you know, when I came to visit you in the hospital, I kidded myself it was a duty visit, that I'd check you were okay and that would be it. But when the nurse told me you were asleep, I realized then that I really needed to see you, to talk to someone who'd been there. You know, in the year we've worked alongside each other, we've never really talked, have we. I mean, we're about the same age and everything, but we've never really sat down and gotten to know each other. It's a shame."

"It's my fault," Cheryl admitted. "I sort of signed myself off the social roster when I first arrived in Courage Bay. I had too much going on at the time to deal with." She gave a helpless shrug, realizing how inadequate her excuse was. Everyone needed friends.

"What is it you want to talk about, Cheryl?"

Amy's directness actually helped. And even though she might regret it later, tonight Cheryl really needed to share.

"I met someone there," she said finally, struggling to condense the tumultuous events into a few words. "We spent maybe thirty-six hours together, and suddenly I'm thinking of throwing everything over and heading back to Turning Point."

She waited for a reaction, an incredulous snort perhaps, but instead Amy sat there, waiting for her to go on.

"He's a vet."

"Noah Arkin." Amy nodded, smiling at Cheryl's

frown. "His name's on the tip of everyone's tongue at the moment," she explained. "In fact, in case it escaped your notice, the two of you are the talk of Courage Bay. How you donated blood, then went on to scrub in on an operation to repair that woman's arm…."

"Beth," Cheryl said. "Her name's Beth."

Amy nodded. "You two made quite a team, by the sound of things. He fished you out of the river, right?"

"Right," Cheryl agreed, almost reluctantly. Noah was being painted as someone who could do no wrong. Well, it was time to set the record straight.

"He won't leave Turning Point." Cheryl took a long sip of her drink. "He's built this image of the ideal woman to step into his ideal world."

"And you're it?"

Cheryl nodded. "But it isn't ideal," she protested. "You've seen Turning Point, Amy. It's in the middle of nowhere, with no hospital, no job prospects."

"So there are no sick people in Turning Point," Amy said in a dry tone. "Are you telling me that because there's no doctor and no hospital, people don't need medical help?"

"Of course not," Cheryl answered. "Beth, the woman Noah operated on…her second child died of crib death, and she's diving headfirst into postpartum depression, literally crying out for help. I'm sure she's not the only one." When Amy didn't say anything, Cheryl ran a hand through her hair. "But without a doctor, what good can I do?"

Still Amy said nothing, leaving Cheryl to fill in the

gaps, to voice the tiny dreams that had sparked as she'd lain in her hospital room.

"I could do my nurse practitioner's certificate, I guess. And maybe somewhere down the road they'll get a replacement for Dr. Holland, someone with passion who wants to widen the facilities. I could…" Her voice trailed off and she smiled sheepishly. "You probably think I'm crazy to even consider it."

"Is that what you want me to say, Cheryl? That you're crazy…that it would never work?"

"It *can't* work," Cheryl said forcefully. "If he really loved me, really understood me, then he'd be here now."

"Meeting all your family and friends?"

Suddenly Cheryl was doubting the wisdom of asking Amy's opinion. She wasn't sure she was ready for such a stark dose of reality.

"Cheryl, like I said, I'm glad to be here tonight, but it took a full year of working alongside each other and a near-death experience for you to think of asking me out, and from what I know of you, your family's on the other side of the country. So tell me again, what exactly are you giving up if you go back to Turning Point? From where I'm sitting, it doesn't look like much."

"I was married. When I say *was*…" She took a sip of her drink, and there was another long pause. "When I got back from the hospital, I opened my mailbox and my divorce papers were in there."

"Ouch." Amy winced, but Cheryl shook her head.

"At first it was a big ouch, but I knew they were due. In some ways it was actually a relief, like waiting for a

dentist appointment or a Pap smear. You know it's coming, know it has to be done, and that ultimately it's for
your own good…."

"Just not very pleasant at the time," Amy agreed.
"Maybe it's a sign," she said thoughtfully. "Maybe it's
a sign that it's time to move on."

"Maybe it's a warning," Cheryl said dryly. "To remind me what a gullible idiot I've been in the past and
where it got me. I invested a lot in my marriage, and not
just monetary things. I carried Joe for four years so he
could get his law degree, and then he had an affair."

"That was Joe," Amy pointed out.

"But I promised myself that I'd never be so gullible
again, that if someone wanted me, then this time it
would be the other way around. I wasn't going to bend
over backward for any man."

"Fair enough."

"He won't give up his work, Amy. Says he can't
leave his business, so if I want him, I'm the one who has
to make all the sacrifices. I'm the one who has to give
up everything and move to Turning Point."

"No restaurants, no theater, no gym." Amy smiled.

"I could live with that. I'd have done it in a flash for
Joe. Would have stopped work to have his babies, been
the stay-at-home mom, but I've grown up since then,"
Cheryl said fiercely. "Fallen in love with nursing all over
again. And as much as I want to believe him that it really is that easy, what if it goes wrong? I don't think I
can go through that again, Amy. How can I pick myself
up again if I fall?"

"You did fall." Draining her drink, Amy smiled at Cheryl's perplexed expression. "From what I heard, you fell bumper first into a river—and who was there for you, Cheryl? Who put his life on the line for you?"

"Noah." Cheryl's mind was reeling as she looked at Amy.

"Just because he won't move away doesn't mean that he doesn't love you, Cheryl. And just because you give in on this doesn't mean you're going to bend on everything. So go ahead, girl. Hell, you can do anything. You're a sassy, bossy trauma nurse."

"You can take the nurse out of the trauma room but you can't take the trauma room out of the nurse." Cheryl grinned. It was an old nursing joke about the confidence that came from dealing with life and death every day. Even new doctors blinked in horror as the emergency nurses barked their orders.

"Something tells me there's someplace else you'd rather be," Amy said with a smile. "Go. We can do dinner another time."

"You ladies ready to order?" Larry was back, notepad poised, and as Cheryl shot him an anguished look, it was Amy who spoke.

"Not tonight, Larry. I think your Touch of Courage might have hit its mark."

Larry winked. "It always does. I'm thinking of taking it off the menu, it's lost me so many customers."

Cheryl was fumbling in her purse, pulling out a note and slamming it on the table, but Amy shook her head and handed it straight back.

"This is my treat."

"But I asked you," Cheryl protested. "We haven't even eaten."

"You can get it the next time."

"Next time?"

"Who knows what's around the corner?" Amy smiled, and if Cheryl's heart hadn't been pounding at a hundred beats a minute, if her mind hadn't been so full of Noah and the road that lay ahead, she might have lingered over Amy's words a moment longer. But instead, she gave Amy a quick hug, then grabbed her bag and raced out of the diner. The warm evening air hit her like an oven door opening as she headed back to her apartment to pick up the telephone and tell Noah of her decision.

Alexis and Ewa were right.

She'd tasted the water and couldn't stay away. Now she was going back to Turning Point.

Going home.

CHAPTER SIXTEEN

HER HANDS WERE SHAKING so much that she could barely get the key in the lock, and if her brain hadn't been so full of her plans, she would have noticed the dark shadow in the hall outside her apartment, would have felt a knot of panic as the dark figure loomed over her shoulder. But even when she did turn and open her mouth to scream, her breath caught in her throat. Tears welled as Buster hurled herself up at her, and she knelt down to meet her furry friend. If Buster was here, then Noah would be, too.

"Noah…"

He fell on her with all the frenzy of Buster, pulling her fiercely into his arms and kissing her cheeks, her eyes, her lashes, her lips as if he couldn't bear to let her go. She kissed him back, the world as it should be now that he was here beside her.

"What are you doing here?" she gasped when she finally had to come up for breath.

"Looking for you." He smiled. "Have you been drinking, Cheryl?"

"On a very empty stomach," she admitted. "A cocktail at the diner probably wasn't the most sensible of choices."

"So you won't be wanting this, then?" Pulling a bottle of champagne out of his bag he held it up and winked as she pretended to think it over. "Buster needs to eat, though. She's been on a hunger strike, and in her condition she shouldn't be missing meals."

"Her condition?" As if on cue, Buster leaped into her arms, growling in triumph at a laughing Noah, who was left to open the door.

"It's very early yet, but there's a bellyful of little Busters in there."

Noah stared at her apartment as he stepped inside, taking in the cool white walls, the pale honey-colored floorboards, the vast floor-to-ceiling windows revealing drop-dead gorgeous views and he understood suddenly how hard it would be to leave.

The apartment was Cheryl.

Cool, crisp, and minimalist, with a few bold dashes of color. The scarlet abstract painting on the wall. The lilac cushions scattered on long low couches.

And though it was a world away from his cluttered house, with Cheryl there, it felt right. She was opening the fridge, pulling out eggs and cracking them into a bowl….

"What are you doing?" he asked.

"Making her something to eat. You said she wasn't—"

"*I've* brought her food," Noah said firmly, producing a bag. "If this is going to work, I can see I'll have to hang signs everywhere like the ones at the zoo—Do Not Feed The Animals, Cheryl!

"*This* is what Buster needs right now, and lots of it," Noah said. "We should think about renaming her, as well. Everyone who stops to pat her will assume she's a boy."

"That's their problem." Cheryl shrugged. "I'll buy her a pretty pink bowl. That'll really confuse them. How's the clinic?" she asked, kneeling down to stroke Buster as the dog ate the smelly biscuits Noah had brought. "How's Mabel?"

"Surprisingly contented—motherhood seems to suit her."

"And the babies? Still eleven?"

"The piglets are fine, Cheryl." Noah grinned. "And yes, there were still eleven at the last count."

"Georgina?"

When he hesitated, her expression clouded.

"She died, Cheryl." He let his words sink in, knowing the news would hurt. Even though Cheryl had only known the little horse for a couple of days, she had been fond of Georgina. "You remember her owner, Mary, got evacuated. Well she died a few days later and Georgina just went downhill from there. It might sound like a cliché but it really was for the best. She never would have been happy staying with me, she was too used to being spoilt and treated like a little lady."

"Was she on her own when she died?"

"Apparently she had a sister no one knew about—" Seeing Cheryl frown, Noah realized he'd misinterpreted, but the chance to tease her was just too good to pass up. "Hey, sorry. I thought you were only interested in looking out for humans."

"Touché." Cheryl grinned but he still hadn't answered her question.

"She was with me," Noah finished without prompting. "Being spoilt rotten, of course. And contrary to everything I believe in, I gave her some chocolate near the end. She slept with Madge, Buster and me for the last few nights."

He shifted the conversation then, reality needing to be faced. "Why didn't you answer your phone, Cheryl? Why couldn't you bring yourself to talk to me? I know you needed space but…"

"I've been in hospital, Noah." The relief he felt quickly flicked to concern as she crossed the room and sat on the edge of one of the long couches, indicating for him to join her.

"I got worse on the flight home," she told him. "I couldn't catch my breath and the cough was really bad. I had an X ray and the chief of emergency medicine insisted that I be admitted."

"Why didn't you call me? I should have known, Cheryl."

"I know," she admitted, accepting the glass Noah offered and taking a tentative sip. "I wanted to call you, believe me. I just…" She stared at the pale fluid, watching the bubbles moving endlessly upward, like the hope that fizzed inside her now that Noah was here. But talking was important. "Since I left Joe, since I moved to

Courage Bay, I haven't stopped for a single moment to really think. I've been running on a treadmill and getting nowhere."

"And now?"

"Being in hospital gave me time to think, Noah. I had a fever and needed to rest, but I wasn't actually that sick, and as much as I opposed the idea of being kept in, once I was there it was kind of nice to be shut away in my own little room and finally catch up with a world I've been running away from—and sort out what it is I want from life."

"Which is?"

"What everyone wants," Cheryl said simply. "To be happy. And I was doing a reasonable job till now. I have been happy. The past two years haven't all been hell. As nice as it was for you to come along when you did, I haven't been sitting around waiting for someone to rescue me."

"I know that," Noah said softly.

"I've got a great job, not a lot of friends but a few good ones, and I've got a life I'm happy with—or at least I was until I met you."

"I don't want to make you unhappy, Cheryl," Noah said slowly as she shook her head.

"You don't. You make me very, very happy. So happy in fact that I realize what's been missing. You weren't the only one battening down the hatches when I arrived in Turning Point. I've been doing it automatically for two years, making sure no one got too close, so no one could hurt me like…"

"Your husband?"

"*Ex*-husband," Cheryl corrected with a dry smile. "My divorce papers were waiting for me when I got back."

"Good."

Noah's honesty made Cheryl laugh.

"Am I supposed to say that I'm sorry?" Noah grinned. "That I wish it hadn't happened? Well, I'm not, Cheryl. It's the best news I've had in a while. How do you feel about it, though?" he added more seriously.

"Disappointed, I guess." She shrugged. "Though not because my divorce is through. It's the feeling of failure that comes with it, the realization that seven years of marriage is actually over. It's not exactly something to be proud of."

"Maybe it is," Noah mused. "You tried your best, Cheryl, and it didn't work. Maybe you can be proud that you had the guts to walk away and didn't just hang in there growing more bitter while you prayed for things to change."

"Maybe," Cheryl said slowly. "I never really thought of it like that." She stared over at him, his long, denim-clad legs sprawled on her couch, that gorgeous brown hair flopping over his forehead, and when the impulse came to reach out and push it back, she didn't resist. "Thank you for coming to Courage Bay. I mean, how did you manage it?"

"I called in a few favors." Noah smiled, and she watched the endearing way the corners of his eyes crinkled as he did so. "More than a few favors actually. I'm probably in the red now— I've got a veterinarian friend,

Charlie, who lives in Corpus Christi. I helped him out a couple of years ago so he could go on his honeymoon, so he's staying over, and Carly's hauling in enough overtime to pay for her honeymoon. I only managed to swing a week, though." He gave an apologetic grimace. "I'm sorry it isn't—"

Cheryl placed a finger to his lips. "Don't be sorry. If you knew how much it means to me, just the fact that you're here, that you came, then you'd know that there's no need to be sorry."

"I was going out of my mind when I thought you were ignoring my calls. I couldn't deal with it. Anyway, it's better I'm here. Some things shouldn't be said over a telephone." He took her hands, both of them, clasping them in his strong lean ones. "I can't do this, Cheryl. You were right. You're not the only one who's not up to a long-distance relationship. It might work for some but not for me. If I'm going to have you, it has to be full-time. I need to go to bed with you beside me, watch you waking up in the morning."

"I know," Cheryl said softly. "I know what you're saying, Noah." And she did know. Those days spent staring at her ocean view from her hospital bed and her chat with Amy had clarified what was already in her heart. She would have told him that but as usual Noah got there first.

"I'm putting the clinic on the market. I've got to get it all onto paper first, though, and make sure it looks a bit more presentable. But I've got an accountant seeing to that, and Charlie's half interested in taking over. We talked a while back about him buying in. I'm going to keep the name, though."

"Keep the name?" It was all she could manage to say as her mind shot into overdrive, the magnitude of his words overtaking her.

"Noah's Ark," he explained as if it should have been self-explanatory. "For when I set up shop here."

"Here?" She sounded like a stunned parrot, Cheryl realized, and when Noah continued talking she deliberately kept her mouth closed just listening as his delicious words washed over her.

"*Here*, Cheryl," he said. "I figure a career move might not be so bad after all. I loved looking after Georgina, and California's full of pampered pets. I could set up my own doggy hair salon." He gave a rueful smile. "I don't really care what I do, Cheryl. I'll even wait tables for a while till I can pull it all off. But I promise you this— you won't have to work a minute to support me. You'll be too busy juggling babies and the occasional shift in the trauma room to keep your hand in—"

"Noah…" Her mouth was so dry she had to force herself to swallow, and finally resorted to taking a rather hefty swig of champagne before she could continue. "Are you telling me that you'll come here? That you'll give up the clinic just so you can be with me?"

"In a heartbeat," Noah said softly. "Well, a bit more than a heartbeat. It took a few lonely nights to come around to the idea, but hell, Cheryl, if that's all it takes to be with you, then it's worth it a million times over."

"No." Her voice came out all wrong; too harsh, and

she watched the hope in his eyes fade as she shook her head. "You don't have to do that—"

"But I do—"

"Can I get a word in?" She smiled at him and took a deep breath to prepare herself for the most monumental words of her life. "You don't have to do all that, because I've already decided that I'm coming home with you, Noah. That's why I was running back to the apartment. I was running back to call you and tell you that I want to return to Turning Point." The hope was back in his eyes, but she saw a flicker of confusion, too. He started to speak, but she shook her head, determined to have her say, to be the bossy, outspoken woman that she was. "I accused you once of wanting the perfect woman to step into the perfect little world you'd created. Well, I don't claim to be perfect, Noah, but I do want to step back into your dream world, make it our very own fairy tale, make it better...."

"Better?"

"I'm going to whip your butt into shape, Noah Arkin." She smiled slowly, moving her lips seductively toward him, teasing him with their proximity. "I'm going to get on that computer and set up accounts, fire off bills, set up appointments, and every second weekend you're going to hire someone to watch the clinic. You're going to hand over your pager so that you can concentrate on more important things."

"Such as," Noah whispered, his lips moving closer, until finally he was kissing her with a depth and passion only love could bring.

Cheryl pulled away, but was close enough to see his eyes. "Me. Your very new, very high-maintenance, exceptionally high-strung wife."

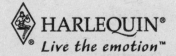

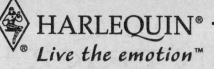

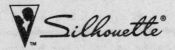

▼ *Silhouette* ®

SILHOUETTE *Romance*

From first love to forever, these love stories
are fairy tale romances for today's woman.

▼ *Silhouette* ® *Desire*

Modern, passionate reads that are powerful and provocative.

▼ *Silhouette* ® SPECIAL EDITION™

Emotional, compelling stories that capture the intensity
of living, loving and creating a family in today's world.

▼ *Silhouette* ® INTIMATE MOMENTS™

A roller-coaster read that delivers romantic thrills
in a world of suspense, adventure and more.